BITTER MOURNINGS

LINDA GONSCHIOR

Quills & Quartos
PUBLISHING

Edited by Debbie Styne and Mary McLaughlin

Cover design by Cloudcat Design

ISBN 978-1-956613-07-0 (ebook) and 978-1-956613-18-6 (paperback)

For Allison and our lifetime of friendship. Long ago and far away on a train in England, you brought Jane Austen to my attention.

PROLOGUE

Ramsgate 1811

"IT IS DONE. HE IS GONE."

"Finally!" Colonel Fitzwilliam threw his gloves upon the surface of the desk and sank into the smooth leather upholstery of the chair opposite his cousin. "What of Georgiana? How is she faring?"

Fitzwilliam Darcy's pained expression reflected the turmoil of the previous two days. "Heart-broken, grieving, angry, frightened." He laid his head against the back of the chair and let out a long sigh. "I wish I could have spared her, but it was necessary that she understood the truth."

"You did not tell her—"

Darcy's hardened gaze met the colonel's. "How close she came to ruin, to disgracing herself and the family? Of course not! She is horrified at the thought that she disappointed me and may have injured my feelings." He could

1

sit no longer and left the chair abruptly to pace the room. "Yes, she is concerned for my feelings, the brother who failed to protect her from George Wickham's scheming greed."

"You could not have known."

"I should have known and taken greater care. It will not happen again."

"We, both of us, will ensure that." The colonel urged Darcy to sit down so they could discuss what had to be done next. "Perhaps Georgiana can spend the remainder of the summer at Matlock with my parents. They are always happy to see her, and there will be no danger from fortune hunters. The company they keep is carefully selected."

"I will not send Georgiana away as though she were being banished from my presence. That scoundrel is not worthy of the heart-break she is feeling, and I cannot add to that pain by further isolating her. To be honest, it would be a punishment for me as well. I will not risk having her out of my sight now."

"What do you suggest, then? You cannot haul her to and fro every time you must travel for some business matter. And how long do you anticipate you could continue such a plan?" Shaking his head, Fitzwilliam dismissed the idea.

"Pemberley will suit us perfectly for the immediate future. We shall be leaving on Friday. I have invited Bingley and his sisters for an extended visit which will provide female companionship for Georgiana."

In a calm, steady tone, Darcy informed his cousin of the preparations he had arranged for the next several months. "Bingley has voiced a desire to lease a house once summer is over and has asked for my assistance in the task. There are several within an easy distance of Pemberley. It should be simple enough to find suitable accommodation for him. Once he is settled, it is likely Miss Bingley will stay with him. In the meantime, I shall continue to search for a reputable companion for Georgiana."

Fitzwilliam pursed his lips thoughtfully. "You seem to have covered every eventuality. What do you need me to do?"

At this Darcy's posture eased, a small smile relaxing the lines that had creased his brow. "Will you join us at Pemberley? You have always been able to entice Georgiana to laugh. I fear it will take some time for her to recover from this incident."

"Of course I will come! I cannot let you take all the credit for her recovery." He paused, then added more softly, "Or the blame for what happened."

BY SUMMER'S END, the gentlemen were rewarded to see the restoration of Miss Darcy's spirits, although she remained quiet and reserved. Being part of her nature, it was hardly unexpected. The company of Mr Bingley and his party during those weeks lightened the atmosphere and made for many pleasant evenings spent enjoying conversation, music, and cards. As the warm weather waned, Bingley reminded his friend of his wish to find a house of his own.

Darcy had not forgotten and brought forth a list of promising properties for them to inspect. In keeping with his enthusiastic nature, Bingley was eager to begin, and so it was not long before he found a house to his liking. With his friend's ready approval, the papers were signed, the gentleman and his sister made arrangements for their belongings to be sent north, and before the end of September, they were settled into their new residence. Larkston Manor was close enough to Pemberley to allow frequent visits for the ladies and for Bingley to consult the more knowledgeable Darcy about the finer points of estate management.

What had begun as a dreadful summer for Georgiana and her brother ended quite satisfactorily. Darcy could rest easy that his young sister had suffered no lasting ill effects from the interference of George Wickham. Additionally, having his friend Bingley settled nearby assured him of continued pleasant company into the future.

CHAPTER 1

Longbourn, Ten Years Later

"HAVE YOU HEARD THE NEWS, JANE? NETHERFIELD Park is let at last!" Mrs Bennet looked in the direction of her eldest daughter.

"It is of no concern to us, Mama," said Elizabeth firmly, her attention fixed on her mending.

"What do you mean, Lizzy? It may well be nothing to *you*, for what single man would look twice at a widow with two children, but Jane—Jane is as beautiful as she ever was, despite being an old maid." Their mother paced to the window and peered out as though expecting Netherfield's new residents to appear.

The sisters' eyes met, their patience with this oft repeated conversation long dissipated. There would be no end to the topic until Mrs Bennet's curiosity was satisfied or her hopes put to rest.

"Is he a very young man?"

Her mother sighed and returned to her favourite chair to address this inconvenient question. "Have you not been listening to a word I have said? He is not too young to consider for Jane. In fact, the new tenant of Netherfield is a widower with two young children. How perfect for her!"

"How so? How is that perfect for Jane?" asked Elizabeth, irritated in spite of herself that a man with two offspring was an attractive prospect, while she was not.

Clucking her tongue impatiently, Mrs Bennet explained. "Jane has a natural talent in caring for children. She tends your children with the greatest ease. He already has his heir and will not expect Jane to provide him with one. You see? It is perfect."

Perfect indeed, thought Elizabeth, sighing inwardly.

Their mother would never give up her efforts to marry off the last of her five daughters. Jane had never married, while her sisters had accepted offers over the years, none of them as lucrative as Mrs Bennet had hoped.

Elizabeth felt obliged to state the obvious. "It matters little how much this gentleman may suit Jane. We are in mourning and cannot engage in any social events, let alone entertain our new neighbours for the purpose of marriage."

Mrs Bennet drew her shoulders back indignantly. "Do not think I have forgotten. I am the widow now, Lizzy Matthews."

Finally roused to speak, Jane asked, "What else is known about this gentleman? What is his name?"

Mrs Bennet huffed in Elizabeth's direction. "His name is Mr Bingley, and he comes from the north where he has a respectable estate. His wife died nearly three years ago and left him with a large fortune as well as two small children."

"How sad!" cried Jane.

"It does not sound as though he needs a wife," commented Elizabeth.

"He must be lonely."

Elizabeth would not contradict her sister, and it would defeat Mrs Bennet's plans to do so.

"What better company could there be than Jane?" their mother concluded.

IT WAS a few days before that question could be answered. Mr Bingley had brought no ladies to Netherfield, and without a hostess, the Bennets could not intrude upon him, even to satisfy their curiosity. They were forced to rely upon the reports of Sir William Lucas, conveyed via Lady Lucas, and they were eagerly—if not warmly—welcomed by Mrs Bennet.

"He has a boy of five years and a girl of three," she told her daughters one evening at dinner. "The children are with him as well as one of his friends."

"At least we shall have something in common for conversation," muttered Elizabeth.

"Lady Lucas has plans for a dinner party so that we may make their acquaintance. Nothing that is prohibited in our state of mourning, of course, Lizzy. You have nothing to worry about."

"I worry more about finding a home for you and Jane than what people would say about us attending a minor social event so soon after Papa's death. Mr Collins will not wait forever to take up residence here."

Elizabeth's own home was not large enough to accommodate two more adults, and her other sisters lived too far away to be of any assistance. She would love to have welcomed Jane, no matter how cramped their quarters, but her mother's dislike for small spaces would make everyone unhappy.

"It is a pity none of my girls married anyone of consequence," moaned Mrs Bennet. "Of course, had Lizzy married Mr Collins when he asked, none of this would be a worry now!"

The complaint had been heard more frequently in the weeks following the death of Mr Bennet. Their home and the estate upon which it sat was entailed away from the female line, the next male heir being a cousin, William Collins. He had come one autumn many years prior, intent upon acquiring a wife from amongst his five eligible cousins. Fortunately, Jane was away in London visiting their aunt and uncle, and for that Elizabeth was thankful. Her sister would no doubt have given in to the pressure to marry Mr Collins and to secure the futures of her mother and younger siblings. As it happened, Mr Collins turned his attentions to Elizabeth, and she very easily withstood his persistence, much to Mrs Bennet's vexation.

Mr Collins, whether out of necessity or spite, consoled himself with finding a willing recipient for his hand in Miss Charlotte Lucas, Elizabeth's long-time friend. It was a match that appalled Elizabeth, yet over time, she realised the couple were not as ill-suited as it first appeared.

Mrs Bennet was far less pleased, for the future mistress of Longbourn was destined to be the plain daughter of her neighbour, rather than one of her own, prettier girls who were far more deserving.

Elizabeth avoided the subject as much as possible. "It is of no use looking back with regret, Mama. We must concern ourselves with our present dilemma."

"That is exactly what I am doing," declared her mother. "Now Jane, we must see what you have to wear to the Lucases' estate next week. You must make a fine first impression on Mr Bingley!"

. . .

THE INTRODUCTIONS MADE at the dinner party at Lucas Lodge were not as dreadful as Elizabeth feared. Sir William did the honours, saving Mrs Bennet the task of pushing Jane in Mr Bingley's path directly upon his arrival. During dinner, Elizabeth was seated next to his friend, Mr Darcy. He was a quiet man, thus she found it necessary to exert herself more than usual in order to promote conversation.

"I have not had occasion to visit Derbyshire, sir. Is it very different from Hertfordshire?"

He studied her thoughtfully for a moment before answering. "My home is in the northern part of the county which is, as you know, the Peak District."

"Very different, then," she said, willing herself not to take offence at the terseness of his reply.

"Mr Bingley's estate, Larkston Manor, is not far from my own," continued Mr Darcy, surprising Elizabeth with this additional information. She noticed the gentleman's gaze was directed towards his friend, who was listening attentively to Jane.

"It is good to be close to friends and family. I often wish I was situated closer to my sister."

Mr Darcy's eyes returned to fix upon his dinner companion. "You do not reside in Meryton?"

"No, my home is some ten miles away, and I have no carriage at my disposal. Visits are not frequent enough to suit me."

"That is unfortunate, indeed."

They each fell silent for a moment, appreciating the pheasant and potatoes.

"Will you be staying for some time yet?" Mr Darcy finally asked.

Elizabeth gave a light laugh. "I am astonished, sir! Have you not heard everything there is to know about my family? I am disappointed in Sir William and Lady Lucas if you have not."

"I do not listen to gossip," he stated, his expression smug.

"Extraordinary!" Elizabeth remarked with a smile. "Gossip is the quickest method to discover everything about your new neighbours, if taken with the proper amount of salt." She saw the corner of his mouth twitch. "However, I think that explains how so little is known of you, sir, while details about your friend are more freely exchanged."

He frowned. "I beg your pardon? To what explanation do you refer?"

"Your lack of interest in gossip is obviously reciprocated." Elizabeth raised a triumphant eyebrow at him.

Mr Darcy smiled openly and tilted his head towards her. "I do not find that as troublesome as it appears to be for others."

Elizabeth's curiosity grew in spite of her determination to be disinterested in the gentleman. His ability to see through her motives only exasperated her further.

"In that case, I shall not bore you with undesired information but merely interrogate you to satisfy my own ends."

Before she could frame the first question, however, Mr Darcy signalled to a server who promptly came to his side.

"Please bring the lady some salt," he directed. The servant retreated, immediately returning with a salt salver on a tray. Mr Darcy placed it next to Elizabeth's plate. "What do you wish to ask me, Mrs Matthews?"

As the dinner progressed, Elizabeth was not entirely certain who was interviewing whom. She had imparted as much or more information about herself and her family as Mr Darcy had divulged about his friend. Upon further consideration, she realised she still knew very little about the gentleman.

By the meal's end, Mr Darcy had learnt that she had two children and that her husband had died prior to the birth of the youngest. As for Elizabeth, she had gleaned that Mr Bingley's late wife had been Mr Darcy's sister, and since her death, the former had lost his natural amiability and interest in company. It had been at Mr Darcy's urging that they travelled south to take up residence at Netherfield in order to ease Mr Bingley back into society.

Jane had been right. The man was lonely and had been devastated by his wife's death. More than two years later, he was still unable to move beyond his grief.

The rest of the evening provided no opportunities for private discourse, and the lateness of the hour when the Bennets returned to Longbourn prohibited any conference with Jane.

CHAPTER 2

"MARK MY WORDS, YOU WILL BE MARRIED BY Michaelmas."

Elizabeth entered the breakfast room to hear those words directed towards her sister.

"Mama, it is such a sad story." Jane sighed. "Poor Mr Bingley! The poor children!"

"Lizzy, sit down," Mrs Bennet ordered. "It is all going exactly as planned. Jane and Mr Bingley got on extremely well last evening. But, what can you tell us about his friend? You spoke to him a great deal at dinner."

"I can tell you very little," Elizabeth replied, buttering a slice of toast. "You probably learnt more from Mr Bingley. I do know that the late Mrs Bingley was Mr Darcy's sister."

"Oh my!" gasped Jane. "A double blow for him!"

Elizabeth looked up. "What do you mean?"

"To lose his sister and his wife at the same time! What a tragedy that must have been!"

"Mr Darcy is a widower?" Elizabeth felt vaguely annoyed that the gentleman had not mentioned that to her.

"Oh, but he has no children," her excited mother related. "Do you realise what that means? His nephew, Mr Bingley's little boy, is Mr Darcy's heir! Mr Darcy's entire estate and fortune are much greater than Mr Bingley's! Jane will have nothing to worry about."

"Unless he marries again," Elizabeth felt obliged to point out. "Mr Darcy may well have an heir of his own."

"Do not speak nonsense! Who would marry such a dull man?"

Elizabeth bit back the retort on her tongue that would only have perpetuated the argument. In spite of Mr Darcy's fortune, it seemed her mother would not view him as a prospect for any sort of woman, not while Mr Bingley was fair game for Jane.

"Even you cannot disagree with me on that," Mrs Bennet pronounced, perfectly satisfied. Humming to herself, she went off in search of her grandchildren who were playing in the garden.

Once they were alone, Elizabeth was eager to question Jane. "Mr Darcy spoke only of his friend, not himself. I must agree with you in regard to Mr Bingley. By Mr Darcy's account, until his wife's death, his friend was a most jovial and cheerful companion. For a gentleman to say that about the man who married his sister speaks volumes. What did Mr Bingley tell you?"

Jane's gentle smile conveyed the feelings behind her words. "He told me of his wife—how sweet, generous, and beautiful she was, and how shy."

"She sounds very much like you."

A soft blush suffused her sister's cheeks. "Mr Bingley and Mr Darcy have been friends for many years, long before either married." Jane's expression changed to one of sorrow.

"Both ladies died in a tragic fire. The gentlemen were away from the estate, dealing with a problem tenant of Mr Bingley's. The fire was confined to one wing of his house, and the children, fortunately, were in another wing with their nurse. Mr Darcy saw the smoke from several miles away. They immediately rode back home, arriving too late to help, only to witness the bodies of their wives being removed from the ashes." Jane said no more. She seemed overcome by relating the event.

Suddenly thankful her husband Edward's death—at home after a short illness—had been comparatively easy, Elizabeth whispered, "That is truly horrible! It is hard enough to lose someone you love. It must be unbearable to be haunted by those images."

Despite the tragic nature of the incident, Elizabeth still found it strange that Mr Darcy had not mentioned his wife, even in passing, during the whole of the evening.

Not far away at Netherfield, the gentlemen under discussion had long since finished their morning repast. Darcy attempted to engage his friend in a serious discussion that had been frequently and frustratingly interrupted.

"The purpose in taking the house was to restore your confidence by easing you into society. It is of no use if you will not make the effort, Bingley!"

Darcy accepted the tiny teacup offered by his young niece. "Thank you, Anne." The little girl went back to her teapot to pour another cup.

"I know you mean well, but..."

"But what? It is not healthy for you to hide yourself away, wrapped up in tending your children to the exclusion of all else. Georgiana would have been the first to encourage you not to be so withdrawn."

"Why are you still withdrawn, then?" Bingley paused to take a cup and an imaginary biscuit from his daughter. "It is not as though you continue to grieve for Helena."

Refusing to react to the provocation, Darcy only shook his head. "I have never been eager to socialise, as have you, Bingley. Meeting people, conversing, and entertaining always came easily for you, and you enjoyed it. I shall get on as I did before, while if you continue, you will become a recluse. I cannot stand to see you like this."

"You would have me marry again?" his friend asked incredulously. "One of these local women?"

"Do not be ridiculous! I am asking you to step out and be friendly, to be the person I know you can be."

Five-year-old Charles pulled on his father's hand. "Papa, come play with me."

Softening his tone, Darcy said, "If not for yourself, then think of your children. What effect will your choices have on them?"

Bingley looked to Anne with her tea things and Charles who implored him to join him and play with the toy soldiers. His gaze returned to Darcy, and he nodded ever so slightly.

THE INVITATION that arrived from Netherfield sent Longbourn into a flurry of activity. Mrs Bennet assured both of her daughters that the invitation was only a means to have Jane visit, as there was no lady at Netherfield to act as hostess.

"Lizzy, be sure to entertain the children, and give Jane as much time as possible with Mr Bingley."

"You are mistaken," Jane calmly corrected her mother. "It is only natural for Mr Bingley to wish for his children to make new friends while they are here, and the invitation is from their governess, not from the gentleman himself."

"And your niece and nephew are the only children to meet?" Mrs Bennet asked disbelievingly.

"It could very well be a children's party with the Lucases' grandchildren and other youngsters attending," Elizabeth pointed out.

"Well, you will mind my instructions nonetheless, Lizzy. You may doubt Mr Bingley's motives, but they are perfectly clear to me."

Elizabeth's children were more than happy to attend the gathering at Netherfield, packing some favourite toys and sweets into baskets to share with their new friends. It was to be an afternoon visit, and when the appointed hour neared, Mrs Bennet was at the door urging everyone into the carriage so they would not be tardy.

Elizabeth was surprised to discover her children were the only guests. Both of the gentlemen were there to greet them upon arrival, and there was a moment of awkwardness, until the excitement of the young ones took precedence. The four children and the governess hurried off across the lawn where a table had been set up with lemonade and biscuits.

Mr Bingley invited the ladies to make themselves comfortable at a second table set a short distance from the first. He signalled a nearby footman.

"May I offer you some refreshment? I confess I am not accustomed to hosting alone and entrusted my housekeeper to provide the niceties."

"Bingley..." Mr Darcy's voice was quiet to the point of being almost inaudible.

"It is a lovely setting," Elizabeth remarked, noting the embarrassment reflected in the other gentleman's expression. "You have acquired some reliable servants, it appears."

Mr Bingley smiled with relief. "I must thank my friend for that. They are from his own household," he whispered theatrically.

Mr Darcy's eyes had been on the children. "How old are your son and daughter, Mrs Matthews?"

"My son, Henry, is five, and Cassandra just turned seven," she replied with a furrowed brow. She had imparted that information during their conversation at Lucas Lodge.

"I must congratulate you on the exemplary behaviour of your children. Do you employ a governess?"

Elizabeth eyed him curiously. "No, I have been instructing them myself and intend to continue until my own knowledge is exhausted. By that time, I hope to have the means to hire tutors in the subjects where I find myself lacking." She awaited his reaction.

It was Mr Bingley who spoke first, however. "Admirable! I am in awe of your fortitude, madam! There are few who could attempt it with success and even fewer who could persist in the face of tragedy."

With a sympathetic smile, Elizabeth said, "My children are my primary concern. They are my husband's legacy as well. I would no more dishonour his memory by neglecting their education than I would neglect their improvement to wallow in self-pity. It is too easy to fall into that trap when a loss is that painful."

"You are stronger than most, Lizzy," remarked Jane in a soft voice.

"I must second Miss Bennet's opinion," agreed Mr Bingley. "I may not know you very well, but I am acquainted with the pain of such a loss. You must be strong indeed if you are able to smile and laugh as you do—and with your father's death so recent, too."

"You will learn to laugh again, sir," said Elizabeth, adding with a slight nod in his friend's direction, "then you may show Mr Darcy how it is to be done."

The second gentleman drew back in surprise. "Show *me*? Do you believe me to be devoid of the ability?"

She gazed at him critically. "Anyone is capable of laughter. Whether they choose to employ it is another matter entirely. However, I must say I have yet to hear you laugh, despite ample opportunity the other evening."

"I fear you have hit upon my friend's weakness, good lady."

"I am heartily sorry for him, then," Elizabeth said with mock gravity. "Yet, I am equally glad for my own sense of humour, for my life and that of my sisters would have been wholly miserable had we not been able to laugh at the matchmaking attempts of our mother over the years. Five daughters and no sons! You can well imagine the lengths to which she would go in order to see us all married."

"Your mother obviously met with some success," commented Mr Darcy rather drily.

"Perhaps with one or two of our sisters, but I flatter myself to believe I chose my husband without our mother's assistance."

Mr Darcy's reply was instantaneous. "Ah, but did *he* choose *you* without her assistance?" There was no mistaking the laughter in his eyes.

"Very good, sir," acknowledged Elizabeth.

"I dare say it would have made no difference. From what Miss Bennet related to me of her late brother, he was quite devoted to you, Mrs Matthews."

Pointing out her sister's tendency to view the world's inhabitants more generously than they often deserved was not in either lady's best interest, so Elizabeth politely said, "Edward was a very good man and an excellent husband and father."

For a moment, no one said anything, then Jane observed that the children's governess appeared in need of assistance when young Anne took exception to Cassandra's attempts to correct the table setting.

Mr Bingley immediately apologised for his daughter's behaviour and set off towards the scene of disharmony with Jane quickly following.

Elizabeth rose to leave as well but stopped, her attention drawn to Mr Darcy.

"I am sorry if I offended you," he said quietly. "It was not intentional."

"I am not at all offended, sir," she managed to say, suppressing her curiosity.

"I am glad for that."

"If you will excuse me, I must see what mischief my children have been causing."

At his nod, Elizabeth turned away and did not look back until she reached the others. Then she stole a quick glance at Mr Darcy, only to find him still standing as she left him, his gaze steadily fixed on her.

CHAPTER 3

"HE IS MOST ODD, IS HE NOT?"

"Who?"

Elizabeth set aside her mending to attend to her mother's conversation with Lady Lucas the next day.

"Mr Bingley," replied Lady Lucas with a decided air. "There is something in the way he stares vacantly much of the time. Very odd!"

"I think you are mistaken," pronounced Mrs Bennet. "Clearly, he is quite deep in thought at those times."

"Yes, of course, but what thoughts are occupying him, hmm?" Nodding sagely, Lady Lucas picked up her teacup and brought it to her lips, saying, before taking a sip, "They say he has never been the same since his wife died in that fire. The halls in Netherfield have echoed with footsteps long into the night."

Elizabeth shook her head instead of asking the futile question of whose they were.

Not to be outdone, Mrs Bennet took up the gauntlet. "He is quite a doting father. I daresay the children are very young and have not yet grown used to their new home. How admirable that he sees to their comfort at the expense of his own."

"That may be," replied her friend, lips pursed in disapproval, "nevertheless, if I were you, I should caution Jane in showing a pronounced interest in his attentions if he appears so inclined."

"But of course he is inclined to show interest in Jane! There is no better match for him in the county!"

"I do not dispute Jane's suitability in the least," soothed Lady Lucas. "It is the gentleman's... shall we say... soundness of mind that is in question."

Elizabeth hastened to speak up before her mother could express herself. "You may rest assured there is nothing wrong with Mr Bingley's state of mind. Jane and I accompanied my children to Netherfield yesterday to visit with Mr Bingley's son and daughter. We all spent a most enjoyable afternoon, and nothing occurred that could be considered the least bit strange or alarming."

"And Mr Darcy was there, too?" Lady Lucas did not wait to hear the answer. "Well, I shall say no more about it, and I hope I am wrong, but it was my duty as your friend to warn you."

"Of course, and we thank you for your concern," Mrs Bennet quickly said, discreetly pinching Elizabeth's arm to silence her. "I am sure it is for naught, however."

"Well, that being said, I must tell you the latest news from Charlotte."

What followed was a speech of lengthy duration, intended to convey the unwelcome message that Mr and Mrs Collins would be arriving in Meryton within a fortnight, their design to take up residence at Longbourn and thus displace

Mrs Bennet and Jane. When the information had been imparted and appropriate social customs observed with another cup of tea, Lady Lucas was ready to take her leave. No sooner was the door closed behind her, than Mrs Bennet began her lamentation.

"What are we to do? Where shall we go? Oh, why did your father have to die, so we are left homeless? Mr Collins will be here soon, and we shall be tossed out into the hedgerows to starve!"

Aware it was useless to attempt to dissuade her mother's hysterical notions, Elizabeth repeated what she had been saying for weeks. "You will go to visit Mary or Kitty for a while, and Jane and I shall continue the search for a small house near one of your daughters."

"A small house," Mrs Bennet moaned. "Why must it be a small one?"

"You and Jane require very little room, and rather than your daughters bringing their families to visit, you may travel more often to stay with them. Would you not prefer to visit Mary and enjoy the seaside while you are there?"

"Of course I would like that, but Mr Collins will be here in two weeks! Jane must work quickly to secure Mr Bingley before then."

ELIZABETH LOVED HER CHILDREN DEARLY, but being at Longbourn, away from their regular environment and routine, had presented some difficulties, and her patience was wearing thin. She had to remind herself that it was not only her son and daughter's behaviour that tried her, but it was her mother who tested her fortitude as well. The arrival of Netherfield's residents had suspended all interest in viewing any available houses in the area, in spite of imminent eviction. Mrs Bennet's remaining unmarried daughter was to be settled to the exclusion of all other business.

Escaping the house to take Henry and Cassandra walking on familiar paths brought back many fond memories for Elizabeth. The landscape had changed only slightly over the years—a few fences had fallen down and trees had grown taller. Her mood gradually softened with the pleasant remembrances of years past. Henry obliged his sister by picking flowers for her so that she would not get her shoes wet in the long grass. Elizabeth smiled at such fastidiousness. Her own childhood had included damp and muddy skirts, soaked shoes and stockings, and many scoldings.

A light rain began to fall, forcing her to concede that they must turn back towards Longbourn. Within a few minutes, the raindrops fell heavier, and Elizabeth urged her children to her side, wrapping her cloak about them for protection from the chilling dampness. This hampered their progress for she could not walk quickly, and it was clear she would get a thorough soaking before the house could be reached.

The sound of horses startled Elizabeth as a carriage approached her. As it drew alongside her on the road, a man's voice called out.

"Mrs Matthews? Whatever are you doing out in the rain? Pray come inside, and I shall see you conveyed safely home."

Elizabeth looked up to see Mr Darcy standing beside the open door of his carriage, while raindrops splashed muddy water onto his boots. She needed no second invitation, parting her cloak to send in the children first.

Mr Darcy lifted Cassandra into the compartment as Henry scrambled up the steps, then he took Elizabeth's hand to assist her inside. He gave the driver directions before closing the door behind him, rain dripping from his hat as he surveyed the bedraggled passengers sitting together on the opposite seat. He sat down and tapped the roof to signal the driver to proceed to Longbourn.

"Thank you very much, sir. I confess I must not have been paying attention to the skies and was caught unawares."

"It is my pleasure to be of assistance." For a moment, there was silence until Mr Darcy gestured to the daisies clutched in the hand of the young boy. "What have you there, Master Henry?"

"Flowers for Cassie, sir," answered Henry without any prompting from his mother. "I picked them myself."

"A very gentlemanly thing to do, picking flowers for a young lady." Mr Darcy leaned forward to add in a whisper, "Did you pick some for your mother, too?" Henry's eyes grew wide. It was obvious that the idea had not occurred to him.

"It is quite all right, Henry," his mother soothed. "We were not out very long. Tomorrow we can get more flowers."

Mr Darcy straightened in his seat. "I would pick flowers for my mother when I was a child. The gardeners at Pemberley were less than pleased with my efforts. Fortunately, I learnt my lesson. I asked them to direct me to appropriate blooms when gathering a bouquet for my young sister."

Elizabeth laughed delightedly. "You see, Henry, even grown gentlemen must be careful where they find their flowers. Be thankful you did not make the mistake of pulling some from your grandmama's gardens." She looked up to see Mr Darcy watching her, his eyes sparkling with humour. The opportunity for mischief could not be missed. "You are so good with children, sir. It is a pity you have none of your own."

"I have not been so blessed," he said in a tone suddenly serious. Just as quickly a wistful smile turned the corners of his mouth upward. "I am grateful, however, for my niece and nephew's presence in my home."

Elizabeth's curiosity was ignited. "I thought Mr Bingley had his own estate. Does he not live there with his children?"

Mr Darcy shook his head. "He has not resided at Larkston Manor since the fire that claimed his wife—my sister. While he is a dedicated landowner and oversees his tenants most admirably, the memories associated with the house are too painful for him to continue to live in it at present."

"I am so sorry," said Elizabeth with genuine feeling. "I am fortunate in that I have not suffered such tragedy and may view my own memories in quite the opposite way, remembering the pleasant moments. That is what has sustained me through trying times."

"I wish I could say the same." The gentleman's voice was barely above a whisper, then he immediately continued in a more normal tone. "I have attempted to encourage Bingley in that manner, but perhaps my efforts lack the necessary sensitivity."

His gaze was fixed upon her, causing Elizabeth to blush in spite of herself. Perhaps noting her deeper colour, Mr Darcy looked away, focussing once again on the flowers in Henry's hands. He seemed about to speak when the carriage slowed and came to a stop.

The rain continued to beat upon the roof, and just when Elizabeth began to wonder if the coachman would ever open the door, it swung wide, the liveried man standing at the bottom step with a large umbrella.

Elizabeth's children were fidgeting, eager to get out. She shook her head and waved her hands at them. "Go on. You need not wait for me."

They scrambled eagerly down the steps and ran into the house. Mr Darcy quickly followed, turning once he stepped to the ground and offering his hand to assist Elizabeth. She placed her hand in his, grateful to have his steadying assistance and avoid the risk of slipping on the muddy steps.

When they entered the house, Mrs Bennet was just shooing her grandchildren through the doorway. She began to scold Elizabeth for taking them out in the rain, when Mr Darcy's figure behind her daughter arrested her eye. Abruptly, her admonishment changed direction.

"Why, Mr Darcy! What brings you out in this terrible weather? It would be a dreadful shame were you to catch a cold." She attempted to peer beyond him, clearly hoping to see Mr Bingley appear as well.

"Mr Darcy was passing by and kindly offered his carriage to prevent us from getting drenched on our way back home."

"That was very generous of you, sir." Mrs Bennet opened her mouth to continue but was prevented from contributing more to the conversation when her daughter quickly invited the gentleman to stay a bit longer.

"I am sure Mr Darcy would find some tea or coffee welcome to warm the damp chill from his bones before he must venture out again."

"Of course, of course! Do come in. We have just this minute set out a fresh pot, and your company is more than welcome on such a dreary morning." She ushered him into the drawing room, Elizabeth rolling her eyes heavenward behind her mother's back.

Jane seemed surprised to see their visitor and appeared equally curious to find out if Mr Bingley had accompanied his friend. She was, however, much more discreet in showing any disappointment she may have felt in realising his absence.

"Good morning, Mr Darcy," Jane greeted him. "May I offer you some tea?"

Mr Darcy seemed grateful for the opportunity to answer a

direct question. "Thank you, Miss Bennet. I would very much like a cup of tea." He waited until she had brought him the cup and seated herself before he glanced about the room for a place to sit down. There were only two available choices, for Mrs Bennet was perched upon a chair while her other daughter sat upon the settee. This left a single chair situated awkwardly apart from the group or the vacant position beside Elizabeth, and Mr Darcy selected the latter.

"I trust everyone at Netherfield is well?" enquired his hostess. She paused only a moment before continuing. "Henry and Cassie very much enjoyed their visit the other day. They speak of nothing else! It was so good of Mr Bingley to invite everyone."

"Young Charles and Anne are also eager to see their new friends again," Mr Darcy managed to reply.

His words were obviously exactly what Mrs Bennet wanted to hear. "Lizzy, we must invite them to Longbourn! If you write a note immediately, perhaps Mr Darcy will be good enough to take it with him and give it directly to Mr Bingley!"

Elizabeth quickly glanced at the man seated beside her. He did not appear unwilling to accede to her mother's request, and although she was mortified by the manner in which it was expressed, Elizabeth was more than willing to make the effort to promote her own children's pleasure in such a plan.

Casting a smile towards Mr Darcy, she stood, and he rose politely in response. Elizabeth was relieved to see the writing table in the room was well stocked with paper and ink. She sat down and drew forth a sheet and a pen, observing from the corner of her eye that Mr Darcy had reclaimed his seat. Mrs Bennet took up the conversation, and her distraction served a useful purpose for her daughter—Elizabeth could write what she chose and not as her mother directed.

With some assistance, Mr Darcy was able to extricate himself shortly after Elizabeth finished the note. She folded it carefully and handed it to the gentleman as he prepared to depart. He looked at it for a moment before slipping the paper into his pocket.

Mrs Bennet saw him to the door. Once the gentleman was safely in his carriage, she began chattering to Jane as they returned to the drawing room.

Elizabeth took one last glance through the rain spattered glass to see Mr Darcy looking back at her from his carriage window.

DARCY ABSENTLY FINGERED the paper in his pocket, his mind far from the object itself. The rain continued unabated as his carriage neared Netherfield. The rain streaked along the windows as he stared out, unmindful of the passing landscape.

A carriage wheel hit a rut in the road, jostling Darcy from his thoughts. He looked down and withdrew the note from his pocket, studying the name written in a fine but strong hand. Darcy had stolen an occasional glance at Mrs Matthews at the writing desk, intrigued by the amused smile that formed on her lips. He puzzled over what could have inspired that smile and shook his head.

Years of association with Charles Bingley had provided ample proof of how his friendly and gentle nature pleased ladies of all ages. From what he had observed of Mrs Matthews, it was clear that her natural good humour and resilient character complemented his friend's in a way that would only bring Bingley's better traits back to life.

He tucked the note into his waistcoat as the carriage rounded the drive in front of Netherfield. Bingley would be full of questions upon receiving it, and while Darcy suspected the contents of the missive, it would not do to deliver it within sight of the servants.

When he entered the house, his friend was waiting for him.

"I was beginning to worry that you had met with an accident on the road. I am very relieved to see you arrive at last." Bingley's concern was clearly genuine, as evidenced by the frown lines etched in his brow and the way he examined Darcy's appearance. "Did you try to wait out the rain in Meryton?"

Darcy shook his head but said nothing until the servant had taken away his coat and hat. He then expressed a desire to warm himself by the fire. He followed Bingley into the morning room where there was a pot of coffee on the sideboard.

As he stirred his cup, Darcy looked around the quiet room. "Where are the children this morning?"

Bingley raised a hand to gesture above them. "They have already eaten and are in the nursery. Sally, the young kitchen maid, offered to entertain them with games, since they could not go out of doors to play."

The door closed behind the footman, and the two gentlemen were alone. Darcy pulled the note from his waistcoat pocket and handed it to Bingley.

"What is this?"

"I saved Mrs Matthews and her children from a drenching on my way back and stayed a few minutes to visit at Longbourn. That is what delayed my return." Darcy indicated the paper. "I would not wish to spoil the surprise by speculating on the contents, but do read it at your convenience."

Eagerly, Bingley unfolded the page and quickly scanned the message contained within. He smiled when he turned back to his friend and said, "Mrs Matthews thanks me for the pleasant afternoon spent here with her children and invited Charles and Anne to Longbourn on a date of our choosing."

Darcy nodded, hardly expecting the other man to reveal any more intimate comments that might have been included. "Yes, I understand her son and daughter found the afternoon quite enjoyable. You do intend to accept the invitation, do you not?"

"Oh of course!" Bingley sipped his coffee, his reply obviously complete.

Darcy tapped a finger against his cup. At last he could no longer keep his question to himself. "When do you propose to go?"

"Go?" Bingley's expression was blank. "Oh, to Longbourn! Well, I suppose tomorrow would be too soon, and I would need to send a note in advance. Friday? What do you think?" He looked to his friend expectantly.

"Does it matter what I think?"

"I meant do you have any other plans for Friday? You are coming, too, are you not?" The question was undeniably innocent.

"I had not—" Reconsidering his words, Darcy began again. "I have no plans that cannot be changed if necessary."

Bingley clapped his hands together. "Excellent! I shall have a message conveyed as soon as the weather improves." To that end, he immediately sought the required materials to put his thoughts to paper, lest he forget.

CHAPTER 4

ELIZABETH TUCKED CASSANDRA INTO BED EARLY that evening. The young girl had been sniffling by late afternoon and, rather than risk anything worse developing, had been whisked into a hot bath, given an early supper, and sent to bed. Henry listened to Jane read to him while curled up in her lap. The house was quiet. Even Mrs Bennet did not disturb the peace with unnecessary chatter.

Making herself comfortable in a chair, Elizabeth took up her sewing. The rain was only now beginning to taper off as what daylight there had been began to fade. A grey pallor was cast on the garden beyond the window. The dullness of the sight only served to remind her that the business of finding a home was still unfinished. In little more than a week, Mr Collins would take up residence at Longbourn, yet her mother and sister had nowhere to go. The urgency of the matter could not be denied, but that was exactly what Mrs Bennet continued to do.

Elizabeth considered the options available. Uncle and Aunt Philips might be persuaded to temporarily host her mother, but that was only postponing the inevitable. Mrs Bennet simply did not want to leave her long-time home, thus she resolutely avoided all attempts to find new accommodations. Nothing was big enough, warm enough, comfortable enough, or close enough to her friends and family. There were a few items of furniture that would be going with her, but until the choice of a new home was made, it was useless to attempt packing any belongings, large or small. Elizabeth silently resolved to immediately renew her efforts to find a suitable home for her mother and sister, with or without the former's cooperation.

Her thoughts turned to Mr Bingley and the hopes that were entertained in that quarter. Jane, being modest, would not voice any wishes in that direction, but Mrs Bennet more than made up for it. Elizabeth acknowledged that a positive outcome, although beneficial in the long term, was not likely to happen in the short period of time remaining before they must relocate.

Unfortunately, once they left the area, it was unlikely that Mr Bingley would seek out Jane to continue their acquaintance, since it would be inappropriate to appear to be courting a woman still mourning the loss of a parent.

Elizabeth was certain she lived too far away to continue the children's visits, even if Jane accompanied her home and their mother stayed with Aunt Philips. There was no sense in holding out hope for a saviour in Mr Bingley when Mr Collins was due to arrive all too soon.

Thus, the mental tally of available properties kept Elizabeth occupied through the rest of the evening. Jane put a yawning Henry to bed, Mrs Bennet retired to her own chambers, and Elizabeth stoked the fire's embers to warm the growing chill in the room. Jane returned bearing a pot of chocolate, pouring out a cup for each of them.

As she handed her sister a cup, Jane remarked, "It was very kind of Mr Darcy to bring you home in his carriage this morning. You might have caught a deadly chill in that rain. Look at the sniffles Cassie had this afternoon!"

"We were indeed fortunate he happened to be passing at the right time."

Jane waited while her sister took a sip from her cup before saying, "I think he likes you."

Elizabeth laughed. "You have been living with Mama too long, Jane. You see romance in every meeting."

"I have lived with Mama long enough to see all of my sisters married to men who love and respect them. I have seen countless friends and cousins marry as well. I think I can recognise when a gentleman is attracted to a lady." Her voice was soft but insistent. "Mr Darcy appears to be a very kind sort of gentleman."

Elizabeth frowned in thought. "He is very good with children, and that is useful, since his nephew and niece live with him."

"Useful!" admonished Jane. "Is that how you would describe me if I were to come live with you?"

"Of course not, but kind and good are not the same thing. Mr Darcy clearly learnt how to manage children at some point in his life. I am not as convinced as you with regard to his kindness, however." Elizabeth firmly set her cup on the table. "We know practically nothing about him, and Mr Darcy himself is the one least likely to tell us more."

"What more do you need to know? He has amply demonstrated his kind attention to Mr Bingley. Now you, Cassie, and Henry have first-hand proof of that kindness. Have you witnessed some behaviour that would cause you to doubt Mr Darcy's motives?"

"I have not considered any motivation on the part of Mr Darcy." Elizabeth then sighed and admitted, "I cannot understand why he has not once made mention of his late wife. That is what puzzles me about him. He is very secretive, and I wonder what it is that he is hiding."

"He may be too affected by the tragedy to speak of her."

"Oh Jane! He speaks freely enough of his sister, and Mr Bingley also appears to feel there is no reason to avoid the topic. It is not as though Mr Darcy has not had the opportunity to mention that he is a widower." Elizabeth raised a challenging eyebrow. "No, it is clear he prefers to ignore the fact that his wife ever existed."

Jane's voice softened. "You frequently admonish me for thinking too well of people, but you are often as determined to think ill of them."

"I beg to disagree. I would not think ill of Mr Darcy at all if he were to be honest about himself and his situation."

"Have you not considered that he may have a very valid reason for maintaining his silence on the subject?"

"If you can think of one, do please share it." Elizabeth looked simultaneously sceptical and amused. "But Jane, why are we wasting our time discussing Mr Darcy when we could be talking about you and Mr Bingley? It is not often we get the chance for private conversation."

"I think we speak of Mr Bingley more often than not."

"That is only when Mama leads the way. Now, do be serious, Jane. What is your opinion of the gentleman?"

"I think you know very well that I like him. I hope you realise that I am not as silly as Mama, though. I have no expectations, and I am merely enjoying Mr Bingley's company. I deserve no other consideration at my age."

"Jane Bennet, that is the most ridiculous thing I have ever heard you say!" Drawing herself up, Elizabeth cast a stern gaze upon her sister. "I would expect to hear Mama say that about me, and Lady Lucas about the both of us, but never did I think to hear you repeat any of their outlandish talk. Mr Bingley would be a fool not to see how deserving you are of every attention."

"You encourage me to entertain hopes of future happiness, while at the same time dismissing your own!"

"I am not interested in pursuing romance. It is your turn for happiness, for I have had my chance. Edward and I were happy together, but my main concern now is simply to raise our children. We are comfortable enough not to want for any of the necessities." She peered intently over her cup. "So, I shall be very grateful if you keep your mind on Mr Bingley and forget any ideas that his friend fancies me! Enjoy the flirtation for the pleasant diversion it can be."

Jane sighed. "Very well. I shall not mention again how much Mr Darcy clearly likes you."

Elizabeth delivered a stern look in her sister's direction, but the two ladies soon set to giggling. It had been several weeks since either had felt easy enough to allow any such display. It was a welcome release from the frustration of their current situation.

The clock soon reminded them that the hour was getting late. With an agreement to work together in the morning to narrow down a list of suitable houses, Jane and Elizabeth bid each other goodnight.

DARCY PEERED over his book while turning a page. With a light sigh, he closed the volume and set it in his lap. "Bingley, what is troubling you?"

His friend's smile was tentative. "I...um...received a letter today."

Darcy raised a brow in query. "Is it an urgent matter? Do you need to return to Larkston?"

"No." Bingley left his seat and began to pace the length of the room. "It was from Caroline."

The tension in his body disappeared as Darcy relaxed in his chair. "Oh, has she discovered your whereabouts, or was the letter redirected from Pemberley?"

"It was redirected." He stopped pacing in front of his friend and stood, looking down. "She insists on coming for a visit. To Pemberley, of course. She has no idea we have left there."

Shrugging diffidently, Darcy said, "Then you must enlighten her. Do you think she will come to Netherfield?"

"I am not sure." Bingley slowly shook his head, considering the notion. "Her fear, she always says, is that I shall pine away and leave my children orphans."

Darcy chuckled. "She worries about you. And," he continued when his friend was about to interrupt, "she was extremely fond of Georgiana. You cannot blame her for being concerned."

"She is just as interested in your well-being. Always has been."

"That ambition was laid to rest many years ago. You need not fret that I shall be inconvenienced by your sister's presence. If you wish to invite her here, by all means do so. I am sure that the children will be delighted to see her." He waited patiently for the other man to come to a decision.

Finally, Bingley nodded. "Thank you, but I shall tell her to wait until we return to Pemberley. She will have to content herself with knowing I am making an effort to attend to her concerns. Besides, she would not come alone, and I do not feel up to a house full of her children, not to mention my brother-in-law."

"I understand perfectly." Darcy watched as his friend walked over to the sideboard and poured two glasses of brandy. "Is there something else?" he asked, accepting the offered drink.

"Yes." Bingley sank into a nearby chair. "I have spent this evening wondering if I did the right thing in accepting Mrs Matthews's invitation. I have no wish to encourage hopes where there are no intentions." He brought his eyes up to meet Darcy's. "You understand what I mean."

"I do not think you need to fear any misunderstandings in that regard. Mrs Matthews is an intelligent woman, and I believe her sister is as well."

The comment only served to make Bingley shake his head. "As always, the mothers are the ones to worry about. Mrs Bennet has made it quite clear that she has ambitions for her daughter."

"Whatever her ambitions may be, I do not believe either of her daughters share such an injudicious outlook, particularly Mrs Matthews." Darcy downed the last of his brandy and stood. "Enough of this. You cannot alter the expectations of those who are determined to view you as a prize to be won. Those who cannot see that you harbour no thoughts of marriage will be disappointed and then fix their sights on the next single man. It is as simple as that."

Bingley nodded slowly, then a grin spread across his face. "That would be *you*, Darcy."

"I beg your pardon?"

"The next single man! The plans must already be underway."

"I have no doubt of that," replied Darcy in a tired voice. "Why do you think I suggested a smaller town outside the range of London to wet your feet in society? Just imagine the stir had we appeared in the city and met with such speculation! That will come soon enough, though. Eventually, we must face it."

Grimacing, Bingley finished his drink. "I cannot believe I

did not see them for what they were when making my first forays into society all those years ago. If not for you, I might have—"

"Stop right there," he interrupted. "The women of the *ton* are not all heartless fortune-hunters. You might have found an acceptable match, but to be honest, I shall be forever grateful that you married Georgiana. She was very happy as your wife."

"We were very happy." Bingley rubbed a hand across his eyes before leaning his head against the back of the chair and staring up at the ceiling. "I am sorry that you and Helena were not."

Darcy's jaw tightened. "You know that our marriage did not have the same foundation as yours." He turned to study his friend more closely. "Georgiana told you."

Bingley shrugged his shoulders. "You did not choose to confide in me, but your sister did. You did not really expect her to keep those concerns to herself, did you?"

"I should never have burdened her with my troubles, but I wanted her to understand. Helena's jealousy was not her fault."

Bingley left his chair to stand next to his friend and lay a reassuring hand upon his shoulder. "I know. It was unfortunate."

For a moment there was silence, then Darcy's chin tilted up and he inhaled deeply. "I shall retire now." He crossed to the table to place the empty glass upon its surface. Then, retrieving his book, he met Bingley's worried gaze.

"Do not fret about what people will be thinking. Anne and Charles are benefiting from the company of other children, and if anyone believes you to have intentions towards a woman in mourning, they will simply have to live with their disappointment."

"Oh yes! I had honestly forgotten their loss was so

recent." Bingley's expression cleared. "You are right, of course. I feel easier about visiting now. Sleep well, Darcy."

Bidding his friend goodnight, Darcy left him and climbed the stairs to the floor where the bedchambers were located. He paused outside the door of the room that served as the nursery, listening for a moment. Satisfied that all was quiet, he moved on to his own chamber to find that the bed was already turned down, his nightclothes laid out, and a fresh basin of hot water waited in the adjoining dressing room.

Wilson, his valet, appeared upon hearing his master moving about, collected the clothing as Darcy removed it, and assisted him with putting on his nightshirt after he washed.

Darcy dismissed his valet and returned to the main chamber. He stood for a moment, waiting until he was sure his man had gone, and he was alone once more. Picking up the book from where he had tossed it onto the bed, Darcy settled under the bedclothes and turned so that the light from the lamp was strong upon the pages. He glanced at the empty space next to him before bringing the printed words into focus and losing himself in the tale.

CHAPTER 5

Darcy awoke in confusion. His mind was foggy as he tried to grasp what was reality and what was a dream.

He glanced around the darkened room, taking a mental inventory of the contents. Everything was as it should be, and Darcy breathed a small sigh of relief. At the same time, he was left with a vague sense of emptiness.

Impatiently, he threw off the coverlet and left his warm bed. The window alcove was cold, so wrapping his robe closely around him, Darcy attempted a study of the garden below.

The sun was just beginning to cast a glow in the sky, the lawn still enshrouded in black shadows.

Darcy's attention wandered, his mind again drawn towards deciphering the images from his dream. He could not remember how long it had been since he had experienced a pleasant one. So much had happened in the last few years.

The deaths of his wife and sister weighed heavily upon him, and there was little left in life to enjoy.

Were it not for Bingley and his two children—Georgiana's children—Darcy believed the despair would have overwhelmed him. With no issue of his own, the future of Pemberley would fall to his nephew. Darcy reflected on his marriage, a union of convenience that had ironically borne no fruit.

Yet, the strange events of his dream intruded on the orderly arrangement Darcy had formulated for himself. In it, he had been happily settled in the comforts of Pemberley, children at his feet, and a wife nearby. The clarity of the images was beginning to fade, and he could not remember precisely what the woman was doing, but he could still see her hands, moving busily with a needle and thread.

He closed his eyes, and her face was there before him, every feature clear and all too familiar.

Darcy sighed. There would be no more sleep for him. He considered ringing for his man to draw a bath. Perhaps that might soothe his tumult of feelings. The early hour gave him pause, however. Coming to a decision, he quickly dressed and quietly made his way downstairs and out of the house. The morning light was not strong, but the darkness of the paths provided concealment from any curious eyes of the awakening household.

The coolness in the shadows worked their magic, eventually restoring Darcy's peace of mind sufficiently to be ready to return to the house.

THE MORNING DID NOT START as planned. When Elizabeth came downstairs, she found a letter from Netherfield awaited her. The fine paper had been placed beside her plate, Mrs Bennet eagerly insisting it be opened and read aloud at once. Inside, in a gentleman's untidy scrawl, was the usual polite salutation wishing everyone at Longbourn well. Then came the announcement that Mr Bingley and his children would be very happy to return the visit to Cassandra and Henry the very next afternoon, if that was convenient.

"Oh my dearest Jane! How exciting this is!" said Mrs Bennet. "I knew instantly how it must be the moment Mr Bingley arrived in the neighbourhood. How fortunate that Lizzy is here with Cassie and Henry so that the Bingley children can be entertained and leave their father to get to know you better."

Elizabeth found it typical of her mother to interpret the situation in such a manner but refrained from saying anything that would be provoking. Instead, she observed that the weather had cleared, and it might be a good day to take a drive and see some of the available properties they had already considered worth inspection. Mrs Bennet was not particularly keen on this plan, but Jane soon convinced her otherwise. The children would enjoy the fresh air, and since they knew Mr Bingley was to come the next day, it was highly unlikely that anyone from Netherfield would visit, thus it was a perfect opportunity to see if any of the houses were deserving of further enquiries.

Mrs Bennet could not argue with that, and following breakfast, she was easily persuaded to dress for the outing while Elizabeth readied her children, and Jane directed the carriage to be prepared. Not more than half an hour later, they were on the road leading south out of Meryton and in the opposite direction from Netherfield.

THE AFTERNOON PROVED TEDIOUS. Darcy had long since given up on the book he had selected to distract himself. His mind was elsewhere. He let his thoughts dwell on the residents of Longbourn.

At every opportunity, he had encouraged his friend to engage in conversation with the lively Mrs Matthews. Both her wit and wisdom would illustrate to Bingley the great advantages to moving beyond his current stagnant state. There were signs that leaving Derbyshire was already having the desired effect. Bingley's step seemed lighter, his shoulders less hunched. Even his eyes seemed to brighten when Darcy spoke of the ladies from Longbourn.

So why does this not bring me as much satisfaction as it should? Is this not exactly what I hoped would happen?

The answer to that was both yes and no. Yes, Bingley deserved to be happy again. Grief had ruled for too long. There was no disrespect to Georgiana's memory in his seeking joy and contentment.

However, in spite of his words the previous evening, there was still a danger that Bingley would revert to his old habit of quickly forming attachments to a pretty face without any thought further than the moment. It was not that Darcy objected to Mrs Matthews. On the contrary, he considered her very respectable and even a good match for his friend had the circumstances been different.

She was intelligent, attractive, and pleasant company. She had experience with raising children and could offer advice in that respect. Bright and cheerful, she was not to be underestimated in conversation, for her wit was sharp and her eyes keen.

It seemed a cruel twist of fate that just as Bingley had agreed to make an effort to return to social functions, the first people they should meet would prove to be acceptable and delightful in many ways. It was unfortunate, however, that the family included a newly widowed mother and a spinster sister. This could only make both gentlemen and their fortunes more alluring than ever.

Darcy felt it was too soon for Bingley to be thinking of anything more lasting than social niceties, and he had been pleased to hear his friend confirm those feelings. London would be their next destination, and there would be no shortage of eligible ladies to vie for his attention. Bingley's confidence would be high by the time they were ready to leave Netherfield and would hold him in good stead to face the onslaught in town.

With that thought, Darcy was reminded of the determination such hopefuls employed. The memories were almost enough for him to reconsider removing to London. However, years of experience had sharpened his skill in keeping over-enthusiastic contenders at bay. Even after such a lengthy absence, Darcy had no doubt of his own success in that regard. He could also count on his steadfast resolve to avoid any attachment.

Unexpectedly, an image rose in his mind, one he recognised from the dream that had so disturbed him early that morning. Startled by the sudden intrusion, Darcy abruptly left his chair and crossed the room, as if to put as much distance as possible between himself and the memory. The brandy decanter was close at hand—the work of a moment to fill a glass and lift it to his lips.

He nearly dropped it when the door was flung open, and Bingley tumbled through the opening with a child under one arm and another hanging onto his leg.

Anne struggled free from her father's grasp, and giggling, she ran around the room until Darcy reached out a hand to stop her.

"Young lady," he sternly said with a frown, "what is the rule you have broken?"

She blinked, lowered her head in thought, and looked up

cautiously. "No running at Pemmerly?" Before Darcy could nod his approval of her answer, the little girl added with a grin and swirl of her skirt, "Am not at Pemmerly."

"That is not the point," Darcy immediately countered, shaking a finger at her. "No running!"

Anne considered his words, her brow furrowed in serious study. "No running?"

He bent down to her level and smoothed her untidy hair. "A proper lady does not behave in such an unruly fashion."

Throwing her arms about his neck, she whispered into his ear. "Uncle Fizzwilly, I *like* running. Do not want to be a lady."

Darcy sighed, hugging the child close. Her words echoed in his mind, a clear recollection of an afternoon long ago.

"Why must you go, Fizzwilliam?" The young girl pouted fiercely.

Her brother put a finger under her chin and lifted it to better see her face. "I must study and learn so that I may properly care for Pemberley and the responsibilities that will someday be mine."

"I will go with you," she stated, looking as though she would immediately leave to pack some belongings.

"You cannot, my little midge. University is not for young ladies."

The pout reappeared. "Then I do not want to be a lady! I want to go with you."

"No, no," he softly reproved. "I shall be relying on you to send me letters and tell me about your own studies here at home.

When I return, you will be nearly grown, and I shall hardly recognise you, I am sure!"

Too late he realised it was the wrong thing to say, for her tears began to flow. "Please do not cry, Georgiana. I shall come home in a few weeks, I promise. It will be only for a visit, for I must continue my studies, but I shall not forget to write to you in the meantime."

"Running is permitted outside, Anne," conceded Darcy in a quiet voice. "You may be hurt if you run in the house."

She pushed herself away far enough to study his face. "I am careful," she said with all the seriousness a three-year-old could muster.

Bingley, collapsing into the chair Darcy vacated, spoke while trying to catch his breath. "My fault. I... chased...them."

His friend smiled in spite of himself. "Anne, please ring the bell for tea. You must all be hungry after your exertions."

He stood and watched as she obediently walked to the corner of the room to pull the rope that would summon a servant. Darcy turned his attention to Bingley, who eyed him curiously.

"Is it not a bit early for you?" he asked, nodding towards the decanter on the table. "Not that I am criticising, but I do not think I have ever seen you drink brandy before dinner."

Darcy glanced at his untouched glass. "I did not sleep well and have had some pressing matters on my mind today."

The door opened as a servant entered. Bingley asked for refreshments to be brought for the children, then directed the man to have Charles and Anne taken upstairs to wash and have their meal there.

When the door closed behind them, he spoke. "Does this have anything to do with what we discussed last evening?"

Darcy's expression did not change. He looked impassively at his friend as he handed him a glass of brandy.

"Your sister? The ladies at Longbourn? I assure you that neither subject influences my sleep."

With an amused snort, Bingley accepted the drink. Almost immediately, he became serious again. "I think you know to what I was referring. Unless I am mistaken, you did not receive any urgent message from Pemberley this morning. I realise you prefer to keep personal matters to yourself, Darcy, but if speaking of Helena is troubling you to this extent, then please tell me. I shall not mention her name again. All you need do is say so."

Shaking his head slowly, Darcy sank into a chair. "How melodramatic you can be, my friend. I have no wish for you to avoid the subject or her name. She was my wife after all. Any regrets are mine and have nothing to do with you or what you may have said."

For a few moments they each sipped their drinks in silence.

"If you only had children," Bingley finally said.

"I have yours to spoil."

"I appreciate the sentiment, but surely you want a son of your own, not merely to provide an heir for Pemberley, but for the simple desire to have a son! Of course, a wife will be necessary for that." He paused only briefly before adding, "Georgiana would have hated for you to remain alone the rest of—"

Darcy raised a hand to silence Bingley. "Please do not be misled into believing my happiness depends upon having a warm hearth and home replete with wife and children. While these things may be appealing, they are not necessary and cannot be tidily arranged in any case. Unfortunately, my marriage to Helena did not turn out as expected. She was not happy... and it is all gone now. We move on. There is no earthly purpose in dwelling on what might have been." Shrugging his shoulders, Darcy said no more and Bingley's original question was left unanswered.

THE CHILDREN WERE IN BED, Mrs Bennet had retired for the evening, and Elizabeth had just bid her sister good-night. She closed the door to her room and climbed into bed, curling on her side and reaching for the book on the table. The words floated unseen before her eyes. Her mind was occupied with reviewing the properties visited on their excursion that day.

Mrs Bennet had rejected them all. Too small, too dark, too damp, too dry, the garden too small, the windows too narrow! Even Jane had spoken sharply more than once when their mother refused to see anything promising in the homes or the neighbourhoods through which they had driven. At least Henry and Cassandra had enjoyed the outing.

Not for the first time did Elizabeth wish that her father had made some provision for his wife before his death— something useful such as buying a small home where his widow could live after he was gone. Just knowing her husband had chosen it would have made a considerable difference in Mrs Bennet's willingness to accept the move.

With renewed effort, Elizabeth attempted to put her frustrations aside and concentrate on her book. Instead, she found her thoughts wandering towards the residents of Netherfield and imagining how the next day's visit would transpire. There was no question that the children would enjoy playing with their new friends.

Less pleasant was the knowledge that Mrs Bennet would be making every effort to push Jane and Mr Bingley together and in the most obvious ways! Just the thought was enough to make Elizabeth's cheeks redden.

She closed her book, gave up on reading, and blew out the lamp. Pulling the blanket up over her head, Elizabeth sought an escape in sleep.

CHAPTER 6

THE CHILDREN WERE EXCITED IN ANTICIPATION OF their visitors. Mrs Bennet was even more eager than her grandchildren. The Bingleys would arrive at any moment and with them, their father.

"Henry! Cassie! Do not flutter about so!" she cried, oblivious to the irony of her rebuke.

There was no time to comply, for a carriage had arrived at the door, and the guests were soon announced.

Cassandra exercised admirable restraint, waiting for her friend to enter the room with only a little fidgeting. She met Anne and a polite but wobbly curtsey was exchanged while the boys immediately set to excitedly proclaim their choice of game. Young Charles had brought his collection of soldiers. Henry was not so fortunate as to possess a set of his own, and the novelty of such fine toys would not soon wear off. Elizabeth was glad she had the foresight to have cleared an area on the floor for them to play their game.

The boys settled quickly into battle, and the little girls played with their tea set and dolls. Elizabeth turned to find Jane and Mr Darcy in conversation near the fire. Mr Bingley was seated in her father's old chair with Mrs Bennet eagerly bending his ear. Elizabeth took pity on him, drawing one of the dining chairs close so she could intervene when necessary.

"I was just saying to Mr Bingley," offered her mother enthusiastically, "how the rain did us a cruel injustice this week in depriving us of his company."

The wan smile he gave in response prompted Elizabeth to speak up. "It is very kind of you to bring your children to visit, sir. My son and daughter would speak of nothing else since your note arrived yesterday."

The gentleman chuckled. "I was forced to keep it a secret from my own, for fear that none of us would get any sleep!"

"Well, they all certainly appear eager to enjoy themselves." Elizabeth smiled, looking to where the girls were chattering happily to each other, and the boys were going about the serious business of troop dispersal.

Jane and Mr Darcy were discussing a similar subject.

"Anne is just like her mother was at that age," Mr Darcy said as he watched his niece pouring tea into Cassandra's cup.

Jane's smile and voice were gentle. "Your sister was much younger than you, then."

Mr Darcy's gaze never left his niece. "Yes. I was not quite twelve years old when she was born. At that age, a new baby sister was a fascinating thing. I spent a great deal of time in the nursery." He turned to look at his companion. "You have several younger sisters, I understand."

"Four." Jane laughed lightly. "Lizzy is the second eldest, and perhaps that is why we have always been very close. As you say, a new baby sister was fascinating, but I must admit that each successive one was less interesting."

Mr Darcy hesitated before smiling, as though unsure if the lady was serious. His gaze returned to the children. "They are so innocent when they are young." Abruptly, he asked, "You must have other nieces and nephews with all those sisters."

"Oh yes! Ten in all. My other sisters reside too far away to see often, however. Perhaps we shall find a home that is situated closer to one of them."

Mr Darcy looked at her in surprise. "You are leaving Longbourn?"

"We must. When our father died, this estate passed to our cousin. He will be arriving soon, and we must be prepared to move house."

Frowning slightly, the gentleman enquired, "Have you found a residence?"

Jane shook her head. "Not yet. Lizzy has a list of available properties, and we have seen many of them from the outside. That alone has been enough to remove some from consideration."

"I can well believe it. We were fortunate to find Netherfield in such serviceable condition. There were recommended properties that were appallingly unsuitable." Mr Darcy looked at Jane with some alarm. "Have you no agent to assist in the search? It is not safe for three ladies to set out unaccompanied on such a mission."

Jane smiled. "Oh, we are safe enough, sir. I thank you for your concern, but you need not trouble yourself on our account."

"It is no trouble. Please allow me the honour of assisting you. My solicitor in London could find a reliable agent who would be able to draw up a list of suitable properties according to whatever specifications you dictate. It would take but a day or two if a message were sent immediately."

Jane quickly glanced in her sister's direction, but Elizabeth's attention was on Mr Bingley. Her gaze returned to the gentleman beside her. "I thank you very much for the offer."

As she paused, he promptly filled the brief silence. "It is a small thing. I am prepared to write my solicitor today if you are willing to provide the necessary details. I cannot abide the thought of three ladies conducting such a search unaided and unaccompanied."

In that moment, Jane concluded that he was to be entrusted with the particulars of their search and that she would write them up before the gentlemen left.

"You are very kind. I am sure that with your help, we shall find a suitable home much more quickly."

He appeared pleased to have made his point, then his gaze drifted to where Mr Bingley and Elizabeth were in animated conversation. He suddenly remarked, "Do you prefer a home situated close to your sister?"

"It is not essential, but to be near at least one of my sisters is desirable. I shall include those locations in the information for your solicitor."

Mr Darcy nodded. His gaze was still on his friend and Elizabeth. Mr Bingley, unaware of being under scrutiny, continued to absorb the wisdom being imparted by the lady beside him. Mrs Bennet occasionally contributed to the discussion, her comments not always mindful of the topic at hand.

"Uncle?"

Mr Darcy's attention was redirected to the boy who now stood before him. "Yes, Charles?"

"Can you please show my friend how to line up his soldiers? He cannot do it right."

Mr Darcy peered over at the battlefield on the floor. The

red soldiers were clearly under the command of his nephew, for they were strategically distributed in the manner his cousin Colonel Fitzwilliam had taught Charles. Henry, on the other hand, seemed to be at somewhat of a loss as to how the troops should be deployed.

"Excuse me," Mr Darcy said to Jane. "There appears to be a matter of great importance requiring my attention."

Jane smiled as he drew up a chair near the boys on the floor to inspect the arrangement of their armies. Henry listened intently as the nuances of battle strategy were explained. The boy had never had the advantage of a father's influence, and it was obvious he enjoyed the novelty of having the undivided attention of Mr Darcy.

Soon enough, the imaginary tea and cakes were replaced with real ones. Henry and Charles eagerly abandoned their skirmish on the carpet for their share of the bounty. Cassandra helped Anne to carry their selection back to the smaller table, then brought their tiny teapot to fill with lemonade. Elizabeth poured from the large pitcher and handed it to Cassandra with a warning to be careful. The two girls were all seriousness in imitating the adults conversing over their refreshments.

As Bingley stirred the sugar into his tea, his eyes were on the children. "I cannot begin to express my gratitude on behalf of Charles and Anne for the opportunity to spend time with your niece and nephew," he said to Miss Bennet, who stood at his side. "You and Mrs Matthews have been very generous. I realise this is not an easy period for your family."

He turned to face her squarely and noticed for the first time the gentle expression on Miss Bennet's face and in her eyes. He was drawn to the softness in her voice, rather than her words, until he realised she had stopped speaking.

"I beg your pardon?" he asked, embarrassed by his inattention.

Her gaze shyly dropped to the floor, her lashes delicately splayed across her cheeks. "I did not mean to imply anything by my suggestion. I simply wished to offer the children a variety of diversions to entertain them during your stay at Netherfield."

"Of course!" Bingley was still ignorant of what she had said. "We would not want to put you to any trouble, however. With your recent loss, there must be many matters of concern. The last thing I wish is for us to interfere with what you need to do."

"I would not have offered had it been an inconvenience." She looked up again to meet the gentleman's concerned gaze. It seemed as though neither would speak, but at last, she moved to a nearby chair and sat, inviting him to join her.

Bingley glanced quickly around the room, noting that Mrs Bennet was occupied with her other daughter and that his friend was now stationed near them. Bingley sat down, returning the pleasant smile of the lady next to him.

"Would you mind telling me again what you just said?"

"I thought you were not listening!" His sheepish grin brought a light laugh from her. "I simply said that Anne and Charles are welcome to visit at any time. You need not wait for a more formal invitation. Rainy days are particularly tedious for everyone. The addition of two more children is less demanding than when Henry and Cassie have nothing to occupy themselves."

Bingley laughed at this even if he didn't entirely believe that four children were not more work than two. As he looked once more to ensure that his son and daughter were behaving themselves, Bingley's eye caught sight of his friend, the expression upon Darcy's face one that he had not seen in many years. He struggled to identify exactly what was different and suddenly realised Darcy appeared relaxed. The tension that habitually creased his forehead was gone, as was the tired, distant look usually seen in his eyes.

Bingley had no opportunity to consider what it meant, as Miss Bennet had resumed speaking. He did not want to appear foolish yet again, and there would be time to think about Darcy's surprising alteration on the ride back to Netherfield.

MRS BENNET WAS DISAPPOINTED with only one aspect of the afternoon's events: Mr Bingley had declined her offer to stay and dine with them. The gentleman observed that his young daughter was overtired and likely to be less than pleasant company for the extra hours that dinner would require. The ladies said they understood completely, and Mrs Bennet was secretly glad to be spared the trials that would have ensued.

The visitors, having been bidden goodbye, now waved from the windows of the carriage as it drove away. All of the children had enjoyed an exciting and busy day, evidenced by Anne's stifled yawns—one hand waved while the other was used to cover her mouth.

Once the carriage was out of sight, Elizabeth ushered Henry and Cassandra back inside. They would have dinner and be in bed before the adults sat down to their evening meal.

Mrs Bennet seized the opportunity to begin her interrogation to determine how well Mr Bingley was able to further his acquaintance with Jane. When Elizabeth came downstairs, her mother had already been questioning her sister.

Jane's face was flushed a deep pink. "Mama, please. No matter Mr Bingley's thoughts or feelings, we are still in mourning and nothing can be done about it."

Mrs Bennet was not to be so easily deflected. "Your father would not have wanted you to lose such an opportunity as this," she began before her daughters interrupted with gasps of astonishment.

She wrung her hands and looked to Elizabeth. "Well, what else are we to do? Mr Bennet is gone, our home will soon belong to Mr Collins, and Jane's best chance for a secure future cannot be pursued because of a silly social rule!"

Elizabeth opened her mouth to object, but her sister silenced her with a gentle glance.

"It has been very difficult for you since Papa's death. Of course you do not mean any disrespect by referring to our mourning period as a 'silly social rule'. Why do you not make yourself comfortable in your room, and I shall bring you a warm compress to ease your mind before sleep?"

"Oh my dear Jane, you are so right." Mrs Bennet gave a dramatic sigh. "Some days I do not know what to do from one minute to the next. What will happen when Mr Collins arrives, and we have no place to go?"

Jane took her mother's arm and led her to the door. "We shall be fine. Lizzy and I shall take care of everything, and you will have no need to worry. You will see. Now, I shall get that compress while you get settled in bed."

"Thank you, Jane." She turned to look back into the room. "Thank you, too, Lizzy." As their mother climbed the stairs to her room, Jane met Elizabeth's gaze. With a slight shrug of her shoulders, Jane smiled wanly and made her way to the kitchen.

ELIZABETH LAY in bed that night, unable to sleep. The afternoon visit had been pleasant for everyone. Even Mr Darcy seemed to have enjoyed it! While sitting with Mrs

Bennet and Elizabeth for some time, he had been surprisingly amiable. This last thought suddenly caused her to recall a recent conversation with Jane.

You are often as determined to think ill of them.

Was that true? Had she fallen into a trap of her own design? In attempting to counter Jane's overly optimistic view of the world, had she become cynical?

It was true that Elizabeth had little patience for the simple-minded people of their acquaintance. Poorly formed opinions and a disinterest in improving their knowledge added to her disapproval.

But Mr Darcy was not simple-minded. He was well educated and intelligent, with a sharp wit that matched her own. Did it matter that he did not speak of his wife? Perhaps she was merely looking for any reason to be critical of him.

Retreating from examining this avenue of thought, she reflected on the events in their lives and shook her head at the irony. Jane had every reason to be the cynical one. She was still unmarried at two and thirty. She dearly loved children and strongly desired a family of her own, yet these joys were denied her. Yes, Jane had every reason to be a bitter and disillusioned spinster, but she was not.

Elizabeth had married well, if not as advantageously as her mother had hoped. Mrs Bennet harboured higher expectations than any of her daughters had achieved in marriage, but each of them had found a suitable match in temperament and were settled quite happily with their families, except Jane.

It was not for lack of offers. Jane had, in fact, refused two gentlemen who had petitioned for her hand. Unable to equally return their feelings, her conscience did not allow her to accept. She was truly a romantic, hoping to find a husband who fully engaged her heart.

Elizabeth had been more realistic than sentimental.

While she had not been unhappy in her marriage, she had eventually come to realise that Edward Matthews, as gentle and attentive as he was, did not equal her in matters that were ultimately important.

Upon leaving Longbourn, Elizabeth discovered she missed witty exchanges with her father. Edward was like neither of her parents. He deferred to his wife's confident opinions, avoiding disagreement in favour of a harmonious daily existence. Elizabeth had felt stifled in spite of this, and there was a sense that her life was somehow not quite complete.

Elizabeth had tried to shake off that feeling, attributing it to selfishness on her part, for her husband could not be faulted. When he died, once the initial grief had passed, the adjustment to widowhood had not been difficult. There was a sense of freedom in being independent with a home of her own, and missing Edward's companionship was not the same as missing the partner she had hoped he would be.

Like her mother, Elizabeth thought her own expectations in that regard were too high. The likelihood of finding a husband whose favourable qualities exceeded Edward's, in addition to being receptive to a widow with two young children, was not promising. Elizabeth certainly did not want to make a mistake that would negatively affect the lives of Henry and Cassandra, and since there was no financial incentive to seek the security another marriage would offer, she was quite content to leave matters as they stood.

Her thoughts returned to Jane and their current dilemma. It was imperative that a residence be arranged immediately, no matter the size, location, or condition. If Mrs Bennet was dissatisfied with it after moving in, it would only serve to encourage her to search more seriously for alternatives.

Mr Bingley's presence was a pleasant diversion—but merely a diversion. It was Mr Darcy who appeared to have some interest in Jane. He frequently engaged her in conversation, while his friend did not seem to be inclined towards anything more than a polite acquaintance.

Elizabeth was not sure how she felt about this development. After all, Jane was convinced of that gentleman's partiality being directed elsewhere, and in spite of the fondness she confessed to feeling for Mr Bingley, there was also the harsh reality that their state of mourning prohibited any acknowledgement on either side. That would include Mr Darcy, should he entertain any thoughts of an attachment to Jane.

The entire situation gave Elizabeth a headache. She turned over in her bed and pulled the blankets up to her ears. It was time to force a decision upon her mother before that good lady also noticed Mr Darcy's pronounced attentions towards Jane.

CHAPTER 7

DARCY SIFTED THROUGH THE STACK OF LETTERS that arrived a few days later, nodding with satisfaction when he saw the distinctive mark on one of them. Inside the folded reply from his solicitor was a sealed missive for Miss Bennet. Darcy was pleased with the thickness of the packet that clearly indicated it was more than one page. The accompanying note confirmed that several promising and affordable properties had been found and the details provided to Miss Bennet.

Tapping the papers against his hand, Darcy found himself curious about the locations. Were they in the local vicinity or near one of Mrs Bennet's daughters? How far would the ladies need to travel to view these houses? Most importantly, was there time to see them before they were forced to make a decision?

"I hope it is nothing serious."

Darcy looked up to hear the last of Bingley's words. The

younger man indicated the letter in his friend's hand. "You seem preoccupied about something."

"Ah, I was merely considering how to deliver this to Miss Bennet." When Bingley raised his eyebrows in silent question, Darcy continued. "I asked my solicitor to assist the ladies in locating a new residence. Are you aware they must vacate Longbourn soon?"

"No, I was not. How did you come to provide such a service? That is rather impulsive of you." Bingley smiled.

"I could not, in good conscience, allow the ladies to perform such a mission without advisement. Miss Bennet reminds me very much of Georgiana—trusting and a little naïve of the world. I am keenly aware of the unscrupulous methods some men will employ for their own greedy purposes, as you must be. Someone might take advantage. Surely, you can see the potential danger and my reasons for offering assistance."

"Oh yes, your reasons are very clear." Bingley's smile widened. "I must attend to some letters of my own, so you will have to visit Longbourn alone today. Please convey my regards to all of the ladies when you do."

"Of course." Darcy was still at a loss to know how he was going to deliver the letter into Miss Bennet's hands discreetly.

JANE HAD to agree that the day was perfect for a walk into Meryton. She was glad her sister found an excuse for them to leave the house, and even Mrs Bennet had condescended to join them. Both Henry and Cassandra raced ahead down the path, their little legs carrying them nearly out of sight before a stern warning from their mother brought them back, only to repeat the escapade again and again.

"I grow weary just watching them!" exclaimed Mrs

Bennet. "Lizzy, do tell them to slow down before they fall. My nerves cannot stand it!"

Elizabeth called the children to her, cautioning them in a low voice not to run so close to their grandmama and spare her some anxiety. Cassandra giggled, but Henry promised very seriously to obey.

They reached town without mishap, and within a minute were at the door to Aunt Philips's house. Mrs Bennet was eager to regale her sympathetic listener with her tales of woe—the imminent arrival of Mr Collins and the dearth of adequate accommodations she had found so far. Elizabeth patiently interrupted the monologue with the clarification that there were one or two possible houses, and it would be but another day before they could see inside them.

Through it all, Aunt Philips offered condoling commentary, agreeing with the heartlessness of the circumstances and Mr Collins's general lack of feeling. When they stepped outside at the end of their visit, Elizabeth felt refreshed by the cooler air. Again the children ran ahead, although Mrs Bennet seemed no longer troubled by their antics.

They were not far from home when Henry came hurrying back, loudly proclaiming that there was a man and a horse blocking the path.

"Where is your sister?" Elizabeth immediately asked, increasing her pace.

"Talking to him," replied her son, clearly unconcerned.

Jane and Elizabeth shared a worried glance, but upon rounding the slight bend ahead, they breathed more easily when they saw the man was none other than Mr Darcy, who had stopped to examine his horse's hoof. Cassandra was intently questioning his every move. As he saw the ladies approaching, the gentleman released the animal's leg and stood taller, bowing politely.

"Good day, Mr Darcy," said Jane as the ladies curtseyed in reply. "I hope your horse is not injured."

"No, no," he replied, shaking his head. "It was a stone, nothing more. I noticed immediately, so there should be no ill effect."

"You must have had the same thought we had. It is a lovely day for a walk or a ride." Elizabeth smiled boldly.

"I confess the sun was a natural inducement." Mr Darcy inclined his head slightly, looking directly at Elizabeth. "However, I did not believe the conditions would deter you from taking your exercise, be it sun or rain."

She bristled slightly at the reminder of her earlier folly. "While a little bit of rain does not bother me, I would rather my children were not unnecessarily exposed to it."

"I beg your pardon," he murmured, causing Elizabeth to chastise herself for being harsh.

Jane quickly intervened. "Cassandra did have some sniffles as a result, but it was nothing serious. Some preventative measures and an early night restored her to health by morning."

"A strong constitution, then."

"Oh yes!" cried Mrs Bennet. "There are no invalids in our family. All are fine examples of strength and good health." The message was contradicted by a brief sniffle and the nervous wave of a handkerchief under her nose. "Come along, children," she added, sending the linen fluttering once more. "Do not run so close to that animal!"

Obediently, they scampered wide of the horse and down the lane to Longbourn, their grandmother behind them. Elizabeth gave an apologetic shrug and followed.

As the others moved ahead, Mr Darcy took the opportunity to present Jane with the letter he said he had received that morning.

"A list of available properties according to your wishes,"

he said in a low voice.

Jane took the letter, noting the seal was unbroken. "You did not look at it?" He drew his shoulders back, and she knew her question had offended him. "Of course you did not. I meant, did you receive a copy of the list, too?"

"No, although there was a brief note enclosed saying that several houses had been found that were judged suitable and meeting your requirements. Miss Bennet," he said, then glanced ahead as if to make sure they would not be over-heard. "Please do not hesitate to ask if you need further assistance. I realise that some of these properties may be some distance away, and you may not be prepared to travel on such short notice. I am quite willing to accompany any or all of you on a journey to view them if necessary."

Jane considered the offer for a moment. "Our cousin arrives in a few days. You are correct in that we are not prepared to travel right now. I do hope these houses are not so very far away so that we may make a decision within the week."

"So soon! Surely, the man will not expect you to vacate so quickly. It has not been very long since your father's death."

"It has been more than three months," Jane softly replied. "My mother has not found it easy to consider leaving Longbourn."

"Of course not." Exhaling slowly, Mr Darcy seemed lost in thought. "There must be years of tender memories and recollections in those rooms. For some, it is difficult to leave, while others find it harder to stay."

Jane knew her mother's resistance had little to do with sentiment, but she politely nodded her head all the same.

"Nevertheless, we must be ready when our cousin arrives, and to this end, I must once again thank you, for I anticipate that we shall need to accept your offer. This afternoon I shall speak to my sister, and we shall review this list." She held up the letter. "Once we have seen what our choices are, then plans may be made."

"An excellent approach."

They had come to the gate at Longbourn's gardens and could see Elizabeth pause near the entry to the house, looking back towards them.

Mr Darcy tipped his hat. "I bid you good day, Miss Bennet."

Jane slipped through the gate and watched as Mr Darcy mounted his horse to ride away in the direction of Netherfield. Elizabeth appeared beside her, brow drawn in a puzzled frown.

"Mr Darcy seemed to have much to say to you today, Jane." She took her sister's arm, and they began to walk across the lawn.

"He brought me this letter," replied Jane, holding up the paper.

"Is it from Mr Bingley?"

Jane placed the envelope into Elizabeth's hand. "Why are you giving it to me? It is addressed to you." Then she suddenly drew in a sharp breath. "Is it from Mr Darcy?"

"Yes." Jane sighed impatiently then quickly corrected herself. "No! I mean, he brought it, but it is not from him."

Elizabeth smiled. "Then it is from Mr Bingley!"

"No, it is not. You sound just like Mama!" Jane took the letter back as they entered the house. "We need to speak of this later. It is important."

She could see Elizabeth was curious, but it was impossible to speak further until they were alone. There was nothing for it but to wait until the time was right.

DARCY HAD NOT RIDDEN FAR before he reined in his horse and dismounted. He was in no hurry to return to

Netherfield.

As he stood overlooking the fields broken up by neat walls and hedges, he questioned the wisdom of involving himself in the affairs of Miss Bennet and her family. Bingley was correct. It had been unusually impulsive of him.

Darcy found little to justify his actions. Miss Bennet reminded him very much of Georgiana, but that was certainly not enough reason to intrude upon their lives. Mrs Matthews intrigued him. She was a woman of independent spirit, if not means, and he found her forthright manner of address invigorating. Still, that was not sufficient reason for meddling in their affairs. Darcy was reminded of his aunt's officiousness, continually directing the inhabitants of her community, and he cringed at the comparison.

Were his offers of assistance any less offensive than the advice of Lady Catherine de Bourgh?

Well, the offer was made, and if I do not hear from Miss Bennet or Mrs Matthews, I shall know the answer.

Darcy resumed walking, leading his horse instead of riding. The air was still pleasant, and the extra time would allow him the opportunity to examine his thoughts and feelings before facing Bingley's queries upon his return. When he finally reached the house, turned over his horse to the stable boy, and made his way up to his rooms to change, Darcy felt once more in control.

"WHAT IS THIS?" Elizabeth stared at the list. She and Jane had found time after dinner to be alone in the sitting room.

"Oh Lizzy, just look at it! So many houses and all within our means! Mr Darcy arranged to have his London solicitor search for suitable properties, and this is what he found!" Jane excitedly explained.

"But how are we to view them? Look at where some of

them are located! A full day's travel for this one," argued Elizabeth, pointing to a name on the list. "And what does Mr Darcy think he is about? Does he go around the countryside offering to find homes for every widow about to be evicted?"

"Do not be so silly! I mentioned we were looking for new accommodations and that Mr Collins was to arrive soon. Mr Darcy was concerned that we have no one to assist us or accompany us on any visits."

"Oh, do not tell me he offered to come with us?" Elizabeth was horrified at the thought. "Jane, you did not agree!"

Her sister's expression became uncharacteristically stern. "Look at that list. We would never have had such a selection without Mr Darcy's help. How could we have known what was available near Mary or Kitty? I have not yet answered his offer of further assistance, but I see no reason not to accept it. Do you honestly believe we can make a decision and choose a new home without help from someone more knowledgeable and experienced in these matters? When has either of us been required to contend with such details?"

Elizabeth knew she was right. None of their sisters had been of any use so far, and their mother presented only obstacles when they had looked into suggested properties. Still, there was something about Mr Darcy's involvement that made Elizabeth uncomfortable. Once again she tried to dispel her negative feelings and to think less suspiciously of him.

"Very well," she said finally. "First let us narrow down our choices, and then we can consider how and when to proceed." Meeting Jane's gaze, Elizabeth added, "And not one word to Mama about where this list came from!"

Agreement was easily achieved as they both knew the consequences of such a disclosure.

CHAPTER 8

Mrs Bennet hardly slept a wink all night, but on this particular morning, the effects were not apparent. She hummed cheerfully while dressing and even bid good day to the servant who came to set out breakfast in the morning room. Her thoughts were on what she had seen the previous day, and it set her heart fluttering in the process.

Never had she considered that Jane—*lovely Jane!*—would have remained unmarried for so long, only then to catch the eye of one of the richest men in the country many years later! Oh, it was too much! The excitement brought a flush to her cheeks and caused the maid to enquire if her mistress was feeling poorly.

Oh, she was a sly thing, was Jane! Never a hint to her own mother and all the while pretending to encourage Mr Bingley!

Well, no matter. Now that she knew the truth, Mrs Bennet would not be unprepared the next time the gentlemen from Netherfield came to visit. It was no wonder

Lizzy had not been doing as instructed—to provide her sister and Mr Bingley with more time together.

The two had been very clever, but their mother was not deceived. It would only be a matter of time before all her plans came to fruition.

IT HAD BEEN DECIDED between them that Elizabeth would communicate the request to Mr Darcy. The sisters had spent some time sorting through the details of the various properties recommended by the gentleman's solicitor and had narrowed it down to four. Those four were closest to their current home and would serve as a place to begin. Surely, they would find success with one of them, and there would be no need to look any further. The letter provided all the information required to arrange a viewing of each property, and it was precisely this for which Jane insisted Mr Darcy could be of assistance. His expertise would exceed their own in evaluating each one. Elizabeth was less opposed than she was annoyed by the need for it.

Immediately after breakfast, she left the house with her children, the pretext of her usual morning walk a perfect ruse that left her mother uninterested. There was no question that the three miles to Netherfield was much too far for Cassandra and Henry to complete, thus Elizabeth's hope was that Mr Darcy might be out enjoying a ride while the weather was fine. If she was not so fortunate, then another means of contacting him would have to be arranged.

It was not Mr Darcy she encountered, however.

Elizabeth was surprised to see Mr Bingley and his children in an open carriage on the road ahead. An excited clamour of children's voices heralded a meeting.

"Mrs Matthews!" Mr Bingley cheerfully called out to her. "It is a splendid morning!" He stepped down from the carriage when it halted, removing his hat and bowing. "I decided to follow your example and take an early morning excursion with my children. I must say it is a delightful practice of yours to be out and about before anyone else! The air is crisp and invigorating."

He turned to help Anne onto the ground whereupon the children set to chasing each other through the long grass bordering the lane.

"Tell me, does this fresh air and exercise tire them out at all?"

"That, sir, would depend upon what they are accustomed to doing with their day. Our routine has been breakfast and a morning walk, and when we return home, they are ready to settle down to their studies."

He looked somewhat confused. "I confess I do not know what occupies their time when in the charge of their governess."

"I imagine you have other matters that demand your attention. My life is quite modest in comparison, even if it does allow me more time to spend with my children."

Mr Bingley appeared to consider the differences. "Very true. My own father had little time available after seeing to the factory business. I received the benefits of his dedication, however. The success of his hard work allowed me to hire others to see to those things." He turned to face her and his expression became serious. "I am given to understand that your mother and sister will soon be leaving their home."

"Yes, although we have not yet settled on a new one." She suspected the source of his information and wondered if she might be able to make use of their conversation.

"My friend informed me that he has offered to help, and I would like to add an offer of my own, should you find any reason to require it."

"That is very kind of you and of Mr Darcy. Under ordinary

circumstances, I am sure we would not be in need, but it seems that fate has decreed otherwise, and we find ourselves in the position of gratefully accepting assistance."

It had taken some effort to say the words, but once said, it was too late to retract them. Elizabeth waited to hear how the gentleman would respond.

"I have no doubt that Darcy will be as pleased as I to be of service, Mrs Matthews."

While the children enjoyed one another's company, running to and fro through the wildflowers and hedges, Elizabeth and Mr Bingley discussed the matter. By the time the boys and girls were exhausted, they had developed a plan.

It was not easy, but Mrs Bennet managed to keep her excitement contained. Jane was preoccupied with creating a list of items to be packed when they would have to leave Longbourn. Lizzy had returned from her morning walk and promptly engaged her sister in a serious conversation about homes to visit. Their mother feared that task would interfere with the more promising work of assuring Jane's future.

As though to deliberately frustrate her further, the afternoon brought rain, confining them all indoors and eliminating any hope of sharing her news.

The rain also brought frustration to the gentlemen at Netherfield. Bingley frowned as he gazed out the window across the fields that lay beyond the garden wall. Darcy sat at the desk, sealing a final letter and placing it on the pile at his elbow. He settled back in the chair and watched his friend for a moment before giving a discreet cough.

"Have you anything you wish to add to these? I intend to send them out in an hour."

Bingley's frown deepened. "Oh, I have not yet read what arrived this morning." He turned away from the window, crossed to the desk, and retrieved several letters from a tray. "I really should see to these before we become too busy with the ladies' business."

Darcy rose to allow Bingley to sit at the desk. He glanced at the rain-spattered window.

"Perhaps it is fortunate that we are forced to remain indoors for the rest of the day. What better distraction from the grey skies than to immerse oneself in business concerns?"

The grimace on Bingley's face argued the enjoyment of such a scheme. With a barely audible sigh, he sat down and opened the first letter.

"If the weather is tolerable tomorrow, we should take the carriage out and drive by the properties that Mrs Matthews and her sister are interested in viewing. It will give us a better idea of the general condition and cost for upkeep." Darcy met his friend's gaze with a raised eyebrow. "You can hardly expect ladies to comprehend these matters when they have not been encumbered by the responsibility."

"Yes, of course." Bingley turned his attention back to reading his letter.

"While we cannot make the decision for them, we can at least advise on projected expenses, which may eliminate some of the choices by default."

"Hmm."

Darcy retrieved the list Mrs Matthews had given to Bingley and pointed to the name at the top. "This one, for example. The name sounds very pretty, just the sort to appeal to a lady, but if it sits on a sizeable property, it may very well be more than they can manage."

Bingley slapped the palm of his hand on the wooden surface of the desk. "Oh, it serves me right for not tending to these letters immediately! If I had done so, I might have dealt with it this morning when I was out. Darcy, I must intrude on your plans for tomorrow's excursion. I may be able to avoid a trip to London if the bank in Meryton can handle this matter."

"Then we shall stop there first. If we set out directly after breakfast, it should allow us enough time for everything."

"Excellent!" Bingley put that letter aside and reached for the next one. "Ah, this is from Louisa," he said. "Both she and Caroline are thrilled that I have finally begun to grace society with my presence. Ha! That sounds as though they have plans."

Darcy grinned. "I did warn you. It is not only mothers with marriageable daughters you ought to beware of but sisters with eligible friends as well."

"I confess I am beginning to enjoy the change. I know my resistance seemed stupid at the time, and upon reflection, I might even agree with you, for now that I have put some distance between myself and the constant reminders of my loss, I find that the deepest pain is finally easing.

"I know returning to Larkston is inevitable, but I believe I shall be able to face it appropriately this time." Bingley tossed aside the letter from Mrs Hurst and said, "You have taught me many things, Darcy, not the least of which is putting the needs of one's dependents before personal desires. My estate prospers without my presence, as I have an excellent steward, but I have been an absent landlord long enough. My children are not my only dependents."

Nodding slowly, Darcy collected his thoughts before he replied. "You are not in error with regard to the responsibilities of being a landowner. You have tenants who rely upon your management. If I may speak frankly, Bingley, your children are very young. Sadly, neither of them likely remembers Georgiana—Anne certainly does not." He paused briefly and then forged on. "My own father never remarried after the death of my mother. Georgiana, I believe, would have benefited from the guidance of another woman during those tender years. She had an elder brother and cousin charged with raising her, and we relied heavily upon Lady Matlock to provide for those areas of education we could not."

Bingley's mouth fell open in astonishment. "Are you saying—"

"I am saying that you should not reject the idea of marrying again, that is all. You are a man who enjoys being with people, sharing your home. The fact that Anne and Charles would also gain from it cannot be discounted. It is, however, not something you need rush into."

Bingley laughed. "You sound as though you have someone in mind! If I catch you arranging clandestine meetings for me with single ladies, I shall be very concerned!"

"The only meeting we have planned with single ladies will be for business unrelated to marriage, thankfully." Darcy indicated the paper still in his hand.

"Yes," murmured Bingley. "Business."

THE FOLLOWING day's weather proved sufficiently fine for their purpose. Immediately after breakfast, the gentlemen set out in the carriage. Their first stop was Meryton to arrange Bingley's business. Darcy waited in the carriage while his friend went into the bank. He was absorbed for some time reading a book, when the sound of a nearby conversation reached his ears.

"There cannot be two people better suited."

Darcy lifted his head, and he searched for the source of the voice.

"He is quite handsome, and Jane is still very beautiful."

At last, Darcy's eyes found Mrs Bennet, just in time to see her obvious offence at the comment. Lady Lucas had been particularly tactless to emphasise Miss Bennet's advanced years. In spite of this, he acknowledged the lady was quite attractive and imagined that her beauty must have been substantial as a younger woman. He wondered if she had been as quiet and unassuming as she now appeared. There was a softness in her expression that bespoke a kind heart, and even though their meetings had been few, Darcy was aware that his impression was not misguided.

His attention was drawn back to the discussion as he heard his name mentioned. Fingering the edges of his book, Darcy continued to observe the women from the privacy of the carriage. He both wished for and dreaded Bingley's return, for the matrons were now engaged in conversation at the foot of the carriage step. To add to his discomfort, Miss Bennet herself could be seen approaching along the row of shops and seemed quite aware of precisely what the stationary carriage signified.

"Mama," she said in as loud a voice as she dared, "Mrs Post has a new fabric I know you will find perfect. Let me show it to you." She took hold of Mrs Bennet's arm lightly, encouraging the other woman's compliance.

"Just one minute, Jane. I have not finished my conversation."

Lady Lucas was of a different mind. "Do go along with Jane, dear. We can speak more of this at another time. I must return home and ensure that all is ready when Charlotte arrives. They will not be staying at Lucas Lodge, of course, but they will surely be dining with us soon enough."

Darcy watched the ladies move in opposite directions, Miss Bennet directing her mother to the milliner's shop a few doors away. He was about to exhale in relief when he saw them pause and look over their shoulders. Following their gaze, Darcy saw Mrs Matthews crossing the street with her children. As Miss Bennet was joined by her sister, the vision tempted him to draw a comparison.

As pretty as Miss Bennet was, he could not agree with her mother. Miss Bennet did not suit.

Not at all.

Elizabeth, on the other hand, possessed several attractive attributes of which Darcy could readily approve. The longer he watched the two ladies, the more convinced he was that Mrs Bennet's opinion was in error.

Their exchange was brief. Miss Bennet soon drew her mother through the open doorway of the shop, and all of them disappeared from Darcy's sight. He released a sigh and was even more relieved when Bingley suddenly emerged from the neighbouring building.

"Forgive me, Darcy," he said as he entered the carriage and settled into a seat. "I had no idea it would take so long."

Darcy shook his head. "These matters are unpredictable. Did you manage to settle the details to your liking?" He put his book aside as the carriage began to move.

"Yes, it was not difficult after all. The price was acceptable, but there were so many papers to sign that I thought there would be no end to it. Mr Morris will proceed with the expansion plans for the factory and send word when I should come to inspect the progress." He apologised again for keeping his friend waiting in the carriage, but Darcy merely waved the concern aside. "Well then, where are we going first?"

Darcy repeated the plan, but his mind was not on the present. He was wondering how further complicated his life was about to become once Mrs Bennet learnt of his involvement in finding her a new home.

CHAPTER 9

"Jane! Jane, they are here!" Mrs Bennet fairly flew from the window casement to call up the stairs to her daughters. "Lizzy! Jane! Hurry down at once before they come through the door!"

"Do not excite yourself, else you will become too ill to go with us," her eldest daughter said in a calm voice.

Mrs Bennet immediately ceased her affectation to consider the suggestion. "You may be right," she whispered. *Yes, that may be just the thing.*

"What did you say, Mama?" asked Elizabeth, coming down the last two steps and reaching for her pelisse.

"Oh, my dears, I fear I am not at all well this morning. You will have to go without me." She fanned a hand before her face as though she were feverish.

"I beg your pardon?" Elizabeth looked from her mother to her sister. "What is going on?"

Jane shook her head, but any reply was interrupted by Mr

Darcy and Mr Bingley's arrival at the door. When they were admitted, Mrs Bennet was all apologies and explained how her malady would prevent her from accompanying them.

"Oh, but Jane and Lizzy know exactly what I would like," she continued while her audience patiently waited for her to finish. "I am convinced that today is the day you will find the perfect home for us, especially now that we have your expertise to assist us!" Her smile beamed fully upon Mr Darcy.

"But Mama, we cannot go alone with the two gentlemen in a closed carriage."

Her mother quickly dismissed Jane's concern. "It is far too cold for an open carriage. You would all catch your deaths! There is no need to worry. After all, you shall be with two very respectable gentlemen." Once again she fixed her smile upon Mr Darcy.

He bowed his head solemnly. "As you say, Miss Bennet and Mrs Matthews are fully aware of what will suit. Bingley and I are merely along for the practical purpose of offering an opinion."

"You are too modest, sir!" Mrs Bennet cried. "But do not let me delay you. I can see you are impatient to be off."

They were not impatient in the least, but seeing as departure would better serve their purpose, the ladies exited the house, and the gentlemen handed them into the carriage.

Elizabeth and Jane seated themselves together facing forward, as Mr Bingley and Mr Darcy took their places on the opposite side. Polite smiles were exchanged, and at last Mr Bingley broke the silence.

"The houses we shall see today, are any of them a more convenient distance from your own home, Mrs Matthews?"

"Only one," she replied. "Where are we going first?"

Mr Bingley glanced beside him at his friend. Mr Darcy answered her question, explaining that they would make one stop on the way out to the most distant property before turning back towards Meryton once again to see the remaining two on their return trip.

"That plan is provided we have time, of course, and that you do not decide that one of the first homes is what you are looking for. As it will be a long day, we shall take a meal at an inn on our way back." He caught Elizabeth's eye and added, "If that is agreeable to you, of course."

"That is very agreeable, and it will be even more so when I become hungry later today!"

Mr Bingley laughed, admitting that he would have been disappointed had they decided against the idea. With a light atmosphere in the compartment, the ladies enjoyed pointing out various landmarks to the gentlemen as they rode on, relating stories from years gone by. The time passed quickly in this pleasant manner until they reached their first destination.

"Oh my!" murmured Jane, taking Mr Bingley's hand as she stepped down from the carriage. "This is not quite what I imagined."

Elizabeth drew in her breath. "Advertisements are often a trifle exaggerated."

"Well," her sister relented, "it probably appears much worse than it is. The gardens are overgrown after all."

Elizabeth was about to speak when Mr Bingley replied instead. "I am afraid Mrs Matthews has the right of it. You see, the overgrowth is rather deliberate. It hides some faults in the structure, and if you look closely at the eaves, you will notice that the roof is in need of repair." He pointed to a suspicious area where the roof met the walls at an obscure angle. As they watched, a small animal scurried out from its hiding place and ran down the ivy.

"I am sure Mama would not like this house at all." As the words left Elizabeth's lips, the front door opened, and a man emerged from the house and started towards them.

"Excuse me, ladies," Mr Darcy said. "That will be the agent we were to meet. I shall inform him that a further inspection will not be necessary."

Elizabeth was determined to be included in the exchange and followed him while Mr Bingley and Jane went back to the carriage. She was surprised to hear Mr Darcy invite her to explain to the man why they were not interested in seeing more of the property. It was not difficult to list the objections, and in light of the fact that the house was to be occupied by two ladies of limited means, the agent seemed just as eager to dismiss the prospect of a sale, given the determined nature of the lady who addressed him.

In no time at all, the carriage had resumed its journey, all occupants once more comfortably settled and Jane already expressing optimism for their next stop. The second house, however, was only slightly more promising with a well-kept garden, but it was a house much too large for their needs. Although Mrs Bennet might have approved of the size, their finances would not; therefore, Jane and Elizabeth agreed it would serve as a last resort, should it become necessary.

THEIR NEXT DESTINATION was an inn along the road that would take them west of Meryton. The ladies and Bingley remained in the carriage while Darcy made arrangements for a private room and refreshments to be served. When the innkeeper announced the room was ready, Darcy returned to his friends to escort them inside.

It was obvious that the innkeeper and his wife had few customers of wealth, but the simple fare offered was of excellent quality, despite the limited selection. Once they were satisfied that their guests wanted for nothing else, the couple excused themselves and left the travellers to their privacy.

Darcy noticed that Elizabeth appeared less hopeful than

she had at the start of their expedition. "I believe you will find the last two properties more to your liking."

She looked at him across the small table. "Why do you say that, sir?"

"You seem to be somewhat discouraged by what we have seen thus far."

"Oh, I am discouraged as much as I am tired of the search." She sighed, a faint smile on her lips. "You must be aware that my mother has not been at all helpful in this task and not because she is too attached to Longbourn—well, perhaps a little bit," she conceded when the gentleman frowned slightly. "I should not hold it against her for not wanting to leave. Moving is such an inconvenience and under these circumstances, it is quite distressing."

"When does your cousin arrive?" Darcy quietly asked.

"Tomorrow."

He shook his head in disbelief. "He surely cannot be expecting you to vacate the house so quickly. I believe you will find him more reasonable than that."

She smiled at the idea. "You may believe that if you wish. Mr Collins is a pompous, self-important man who will be only too happy to inform you of his irreplaceable value."

The description of the gentleman seemed vaguely familiar to Darcy. His mind sought out the connexion even as he continued to listen to Elizabeth speak.

"His presence alone should be more than enough incentive for our mother to accept a smaller home or at the very least to visit one of her daughters for a while."

"And that would allow you the time required to come to an agreement and facilitate the move."

"I know it sounds rather calculating, but it is in fact kinder and spares her the pain of worrying about how everything will be accomplished." She glanced to where her sister and Bingley were engrossed in their own conversation, then she turned her attention back to her companion. "I should like to ask you a question, sir."

Surprised, he leaned back and with a look invited her to speak.

"At our very first meeting, sir, you revealed that your purpose in coming to Netherfield was to help your friend re-enter the social sphere. Do you believe you have met with some success?"

There was a challenge in her raised eyebrow that Darcy could not ignore. "Yes, I do."

Her smile warmed. "And what of yourself?"

He blinked. "What do you mean?"

"Are you sufficiently prepared for the demands society will inflict once you return to your home, or perhaps you will venture on to London?"

"I am as prepared as I have always been, which is to say that all efforts to secure me will be in vain." Pausing to take stock of Bingley's progress, Darcy was about to comment further when the lady spoke first.

"How is it then, if you were always of the mind to deflect such efforts, there was ever a Mrs Darcy at all?" The sparkle in her eyes took the sting from her words.

A smile touched his lips. "You assume with such a question that I have never desired to marry, when, in fact, what I said was that the efforts of others to lure me into the state would not meet with success."

She was clearly not ready to concede yet. "Then I must beg to presume again and conclude that once you have set your mind on something, you do not rest until you have achieved your goal." His expression must have reflected puzzlement for she explained further.

"If you were unmoved by the sometimes herculean efforts of single ladies and their matchmaking mothers, then I was naturally drawn to believe you had chosen a less determined belle and pursued her until she agreed to marry you."

Darcy opened his mouth, then shut it again. Finally, he managed to say, "I fail to follow your reasoning. That is quite a leap in logic."

"Oh, you did not think me serious, did you? I know nothing of your late wife and barely anything about yourself."

"Then I shall put your mind at ease." He leaned forward to speak more quietly. "Our courtship was nothing of the sort you have suggested, nor am I offended by the manner you chose to satisfy your curiosity." As the colour rose in her cheeks, Darcy felt himself grow warm as well. "In keeping with our stations, my wife and I were well suited in many respects. There was no scandal, no broken hearts, or romantic trysts. It was a match agreeable to all parties."

"All parties?" Elizabeth repeated in a harsh whisper.

"Our families," he said with little indication that it would have mattered.

A polite cough from the other end of the table startled them both into silence. As flush climbed further up the lady's face, Darcy looked away to ask Bingley, "Are we ready to leave now?"

"We are." Bingley opened the door and waited for Miss Bennet to pass through, then announced to the other couple, "I shall inform the driver we shall be leaving shortly."

They were gone before Darcy could rise from his seat.

ELIZABETH scarcely hesitated before placing her fingers onto Mr Darcy's palm when he offered it.

She turned to face him and was struck by his intent expression. His eyes were bright, almost questioning. Elizabeth heard herself say something senseless before looking away, then almost immediately stole a glance as he walked beside her.

Admitting that Mr Darcy was undeniably handsome, his features strong and well defined, it was not difficult for her to extend that admiration to his character. Despite her initial irritation at his offer of assistance, Elizabeth recognised the advantage in his better knowledge and experience, and was grateful for Jane's sensible decision to accept.

Outside, the fresh air brought Elizabeth's attention to the present. Mr Darcy excused himself to settle their bill with the innkeeper. Mr Bingley was at the carriage step to hand her up, and Jane paid no special attention when her sister sat beside her. The gentlemen joined them a few minutes later and signalled the driver to move on.

Jane and Mr Bingley immediately began conversing, about what Elizabeth could not say. She was more interested in contemplating the new information she had drawn from Mr Darcy, and wondered again how he managed to convey so little even when answering a direct question.

The gentleman himself was quieter than usual. He had at first responded once or twice to his friend's comments but then lapsed into silence and became engrossed in a serious study of the passing countryside.

By the time they reached their next destination, Elizabeth had put aside her preoccupation. Jane seemed to listen more to Mr Bingley's advice than petition her sister for explanations, and Mr Darcy was never far away for another opinion.

The final house inspection was more fruitful. Both Elizabeth and Jane were convinced they had at last found the right place—a home of which Mrs Bennet would approve, but most of all, one they could afford. The gentlemen agreed that the house and property would not harbour any unpleasant surprises. All that remained was to obtain Mrs Bennet's agreement, something that should not prove difficult, once

Jane presented the idea. Then they would engage a solicitor to begin the tedious legal process.

The mood of the foursome was much lighter on the trip back to Longbourn than when they left that morning. Laughter sent tension fleeing, and without any conscious thought, they had settled into their seats—Jane and Mr Bingley on one side, Mr Darcy and Elizabeth on the other.

CHAPTER 10

REVEREND WILLIAM COLLINS CONSIDERED HIMSELF a patient man. It was a necessary attribute for his chosen profession and for his patroness. The grand Lady Catherine de Bourgh would abide no less than the patience of a saint in anyone. In the years he had spent tending his flock at Hunsford, Mr Collins had also seen fit to increase the numbers in the parish by the addition of a wife and four children. Mrs Collins, formerly of Meryton, was a long-time girlhood friend of his cousin Elizabeth Bennet, now Mrs Matthews. Charlotte Collins and Elizabeth had shared opinions—often opposed—and letters when their children were born and as they grew. Naturally, these exchanges became less frequent as their lives became busier.

The tragic loss of Elizabeth's father brought Mrs Collins home again, if not to her own family's house, at least to the area. Her husband could not entirely conceal his excitement in his elevated status. Longbourn may not have been an estate of enormous proportions, but it was now his own to oversee and bring to prosperity so that his sons might reap the benefits upon his death.

ELIZABETH AND JANE were expecting the imminent arrival of Mr Bingley and Mr Darcy to help begin the process of purchasing the house they had decided upon, when Mr Collins's carriage pulled up to their doorstep. His arrival was inconvenient at best.

Charlotte was lost in the rush of children descending from the carriage, and Elizabeth patiently waited for her to emerge, warmly greeting her friend with an embrace.

"It has been too long since we last met, Charlotte. My, how the boys have grown!"

The children were busily expending pent up energy by racing across the lawn and through the gardens. Elizabeth marvelled at how all of them had fit inside the compartment with their parents.

"You look very well, Eliza." As Charlotte spoke she kept her eyes on the progress of her children. "The last few months must have been difficult. I am sorry there was so little time for Jane and your mother to arrange things. What have you managed? Is there anything I can do to help?"

"Thank you, no," replied Elizabeth with a smile. "We have just yesterday found a house, and this afternoon we shall see to the particulars."

"My goodness! I am impressed."

Any further comments were interrupted by an urgent summons from her husband to come inside and out of the sun.

Mrs Bennet had earlier ensured that refreshments would be ready at a moment's notice; therefore, the sitting room table was already brimming with tea, coffee, and cakes as she calmly invited her guests inside and offered them their choice from the selection.

As soon as Mr Collins opened his mouth to speak, Elizabeth sighed to herself, remembering her earlier description of the man, and wishing more than ever for the presence of her father, so they could, as before, share their amusement at the spectacle he made.

"ABSOLUTELY NOT!"

Darcy blinked in surprise, his foot nearly missing the stirrup. As he swung himself into the saddle, he waited for his friend to expound upon his outburst.

"I am not going to expose my children to the atmosphere in London," Bingley continued most stridently. "They have made friends here and are enjoying themselves. I am enjoying our time here as well. If you feel inclined to go to town, by all means go! Anne, Charles, and I are staying here." With a flick of its tail, his horse was away across the lawn.

When Darcy finally drew up alongside his friend and both horses slowed to a walk, he commented, "I had no idea you felt so strongly about it. When did your opinion of London change?"

"I cannot say exactly." Bingley considered the question. "It was only when you suggested we go there that I realised how much I disliked the city. Oh, I used to enjoy being there when I was young and knew no better, but the years in the north have spoiled me with a greater appreciation for clean air, space, and quiet." He gestured to the open land around them.

"I cannot disagree with you."

"You encouraged me to put my children's needs first, and that is precisely what I am doing. They are too young to understand the educational and social aspects of town life. I know it cannot be avoided forever, but while I can, I shall protect them from the less attractive influences found there."

Darcy nodded slowly. "I commend you for your efforts, Bingley. It certainly will not be any easier as they grow older, but your diligence at this age will prove beneficial."

He said nothing more for a moment or two and studied the trees in the distance. When he finally spoke again, Darcy turned to face his friend squarely.

"I have no wish to travel to London. I was more concerned that you may not find enough here to interest you, and although it has been fortuitous to find friends for Anne and Charles, that was not the aim in taking Netherfield and leaving Pemberley behind. I admit I pushed you into the social sphere and that my intent was for you to once more be the Bingley we both remember. There has been progress, of course, but I cannot help but feel I have been less than successful in my efforts."

"Good Lord, Darcy! I am not the foolish young man of ten years ago! Unlike then, I am perfectly aware of the expectations circling us like vultures. Oh, that is a poor analogy I know, but you need not worry that I shall quickly succumb to the charming company we have been keeping merely because I had behaved that way in the past. I heard your message the other day loud and clear. If and when I do entertain thoughts of remarrying, it will be on my own terms, not to satisfy someone else's idea of what that should be and certainly not because I am blinded by a pretty face."

Darcy looked at him with a newfound understanding. "I realise that now, and I apologise for underestimating you. It is my own fault, of course. I have repeatedly encouraged you to seek out the company and conversation to be found at Longbourn, to reciprocate by invitations to visit there under the pretext of increased social exposure for Anne and

Charles. I would have only myself to blame had you formed an attachment with Mrs Matthews."

Bingley halted his horse, his expression pure astonishment. "Mrs Matthews? You believed me to be interested in *Mrs Matthews?*"

Darcy circled his horse around to where Bingley's horse stood. "Why, yes," he responded, somewhat puzzled. "I suggested as much often enough. She has two children of her own and the knowledge and experience to assist with yours. Mrs Matthews would make a good match for you."

The reins nearly slipped from Bingley's grasp. "To be perfectly honest, Darcy, I think she would make a better match for you!"

"Me!" His shock was all the greater for hearing the other man's words echoing his own thoughts, and his fingers twitched on the reins, causing his horse to sidestep nervously.

"Yes, you. Mrs Matthews is intelligent, well-read, converses easily, and has manners that are pleasing. I think she would make an excellent match for you."

Darcy's spine stiffened. "I have not the smallest intention of seeking a match," he managed to utter and was appalled at the way it sounded when it reached his ears.

Bingley grinned. "So you keep saying. Is that why you suggested running off to town? You thought I was interested in the lady and did not want to get in my way—or is your control slipping?"

Shaking his head, Darcy grumbled, "Is it me or are you making less sense than usual?"

Bingley merely chuckled then urged his horse forward, looking over his shoulder to say, "At least consider the idea, my friend. I know you will see that I am right."

It is all too easy to convince myself of that, thought Darcy.

. . .

UPON ENTERING Longbourn's sitting room, Darcy immediately recognised the gentleman introduced as Mr Collins. His aunt's sycophantic parson was not only a familiar but an unwelcome sight. He had been privy to personal and unpleasant events that had occurred between Lady Catherine de Bourgh and himself, and had demonstrated no desire to curb his tongue in broadcasting his aunt's opinions regarding them.

This is the man forcing the ladies out of Longbourn. Elizabeth's description of him was generous. Darcy's distaste for the situation and for Collins increased.

The introductions were acknowledged with a nod from Darcy, but the other man puffed out his chest and tilted his chin upward in a disrespectful manner. Ignoring him, Darcy bowed and addressed the lady behind him.

"Mrs Collins, it is a pleasure to see you again. I trust your family is well."

Mrs Collins curtseyed, her eyes briefly turned in her husband's direction. "Thank you, sir. They are all well."

The ladies took their seats, Bingley quickly choosing to sit near Jane. Darcy was not pleased to see his only option was next to Mr Collins. Almost as quickly, he realised Elizabeth was seated on the other side of the vacant chair. His hesitation vanished upon seeing her welcoming smile and a clear invitation conveyed in her eyes. He took his place and deliberately positioned himself to face the lady, his back towards her cousin.

An awkward silence persisted for a moment, until Mrs Bennet spoke.

"As I was just telling Mr and Mrs Collins, we would never have found such a perfect new home without your assistance." She smiled and nodded at Darcy and Bingley. "I am now quite excited at the prospect of moving!"

A quiet sigh beside him brought Darcy's gaze back to

Elizabeth. He gave her a sympathetic smile and was heartened to see her lips respond in kind.

"You must be careful, madam, where you seek advice and assistance," Mr Collins offered.

"I do not understand you, sir. What do you mean?" Despite the question, Mrs Bennet's countenance did not suggest she was receptive to any advice.

The clergyman affected an air of one correcting a child. "I fear you may have been deceived into believing the offer of assistance was not without other motivations."

There were gasps throughout the room. Darcy turned in his chair to face Mr Collins directly, not bothering to disguise his growing anger.

"I say no more or less than Lady Catherine de Bourgh, this gentleman's esteemed aunt, would say if she were here. How she withstood the offence to herself and her daughter, Miss Anne de Bourgh, is a tribute to her fine and noble person."

"I say," cried Bingley, unable to remain silent any longer. "There is no call to slander my friend's character in this way! Darcy has done nothing to deserve such censure."

Mr Collins sniffed disdainfully. "If you were acquainted with the facts—"

"Facts, like truths, are often dependent upon the individual relating them," interrupted Elizabeth in a tone that brooked no argument. "Thank you for your concern, Mr Collins, but in our short acquaintance with Mr Darcy and Mr Bingley, we have been assured of their steadfast and excellent characters. It is unfortunate that your patroness had a disagreement with her nephew, for it is very often true that those sad circumstances will colour one's opinion and lead to a distorted view. But I am sure there is no need to remind you of that, sir, for you must have counselled many of your parishioners to successful resolutions of similar incidents in their own family households."

Her speech left her cousin with mouth agape but no words issued forth.

Darcy stared in open admiration of the lady. She could not possibly know how close her words were to the truth, and he was gratified by the trust implicit in her statements.

"Mr Collins, Lady Catherine exercised her choice to disclose such personal matters beyond the family circle, but I must ask that you refrain from spreading them further. While my aunt and I did not agree on the subject, it in no way lessens the respect I would have her shown, both by myself and others. This also extends to my late cousin. I will not have the tale spread far and wide like idle gossip."

At the mention of gossip, Mr Collins blanched and stuttered an apology. "I...I understand you perfectly, Mr Darcy. I shall say no more on the subject."

Darcy was satisfied for the moment, but he knew he must take the first opportunity to explain to Elizabeth what had happened to set his aunt so decidedly against him. It was suddenly of vital importance to secure her continued trust, and in spite of her words to Mr Collins, Darcy was not assured that her confidence in him had not suffered a blow.

Bingley suggested it was time they remove to a quieter room where the details of the sale of the house could be discussed privately.

"Of course," agreed Miss Bennet. "Our father's study is the perfect place." She turned to her sister and said, "Let us go into Father's book room so we do not disturb the others."

Mrs Bennet remained in the sitting room with Mr and Mrs Collins. She proclaimed herself to be a fountain of information about running the house, something Mrs Collins must surely learn.

As Bingley opened the door to leave, a tangle of the

Collins's children fell through and into the sitting room. The resulting noise only served to accelerate the exit of the two ladies and Bingley. Darcy paused, stared intently at Mr Collins to impress his displeasure upon the man, then followed the others out of the room.

CHAPTER 11

Two days later, Mr Bingley spied Miss Bennet in Meryton while on his way through the village in his carriage and quickly called to his driver to stop. He called out to her upon setting foot on the ground.

She looked up and smiled warmly. "Good afternoon, Mr Bingley. What brings you to town today?"

"I had some business at the bank. Tell me, how are the moving arrangements progressing?"

"Very well. My mother has thrown herself into organising what will be brought with us and what will stay. We cannot thank you and Mr Darcy enough for what you have done to make this so much easier. Soon the worst will be over, and in another two weeks, my mother and I shall be settling into our new home."

"It was a pleasure to be of assistance." Mr Bingley bowed his head politely. "Please give my regards to your mother and sister. I hope to see you all again soon."

"Oh, Lizzy went home this morning with her children. She will not be able to return before we leave Longbourn. I shall, of course, send your regards in my next letter to her."

"What a surprise! We had no idea Mrs Matthews intended to leave so soon."

"None of us did." Jane stepped a bit closer to speak more quietly. "Longbourn is not so large a house that the addition of four children was not keenly felt. It was unfortunate, but Lizzy decided it best that she leave with Cassandra and Henry sooner rather than later. Mr Collins was kind enough to lend her his carriage for the trip."

"That was most gracious of him."

"Yes." Jane did not elaborate. "I am sorry that Anne and Charles will not have the enjoyment of their friends' company now."

"I daresay there will be some disappointment when I relate the news."

"Once we are settled into our new home, I know Lizzy will come with her children, and they can see one another again."

"That is true, since I have no intention of leaving Netherfield." He looked away. "Well, I had best not detain you any longer. You must have many things to—"

Jane quietly interrupted. "I shall be sure to convey your greetings to my mother and Lizzy. Please give my regards to your children and Mr Darcy."

"I shall!" Mr Bingley tipped his hat and turned back towards his waiting carriage. "I say, are you on your way back to Longbourn? May I offer you a ride?"

"Thank you, sir. I have finished my errands, and I am grateful to accept your kind offer."

. . .

DARCY FINISHED his meal and set his fork down beside his plate. "You will be obliged to accept some of those invitations now, I presume, unless you have found a means of escape through some other excuse."

Bingley frowned at his friend. "I do not need an excuse. And what do you mean I shall feel obliged to accept them *now*?"

"Now that a visit to Longbourn is out of the question."

"Yes, of course. I have no desire to spend an hour with Collins, no matter whose aunt may recommend him."

Darcy laughed at that. "Lady Catherine has a unique perspective. I doubt there are many she would recommend."

"Including yourself, apparently."

Shaking his head, Darcy sighed. "That is a long and complicated story."

From the expression on the other man's face, Bingley knew it was a subject best not pursued. "Perhaps a quiet afternoon or two would be desirable. I did learn something from Mrs Matthews that I may put into practice starting today."

Curiosity prompted Darcy to ask, "To what do you refer?"

"Exercise! Walking and running and fresh air."

Darcy stared at him incredulously. "You intend to run around out of doors? You cannot be serious! What purpose will that serve? I find it difficult to believe Mrs Matthews would suggest such a thing!" Darcy appeared even more frustrated when Bingley laughed at his objections. "What is so amusing?"

"If you could only see your face, Darcy!" Bingley managed to control himself enough to explain. "I have not lost my mind. You need not fear for the sanity of Mrs Matthews either. The fresh air and running is for Anne and Charles, not me. Tiring them out, I have been assured, is the key to a peaceful existence."

"There is one small thing you have forgotten." Darcy leaned forward, his hands resting on the table. "Mrs Matthews does not have the advantage of a governess to entertain her children. You do. She cannot send them off with a servant to tend to other matters uninterrupted. You have that opportunity. That is why she needed to find a method to ensure some quiet for her to fulfil her other responsibilities."

"You may be right, but that does not make it any less beneficial for the children. Therefore, I remain determined to make the effort."

Darcy had nothing further to say except to wish his friend pleasure on the outing, for he preferred to stay inside in quiet solitude. There were some important matters to be very carefully considered. That was something that could not be done with children underfoot and a talkative Bingley in attendance.

It was at least an hour later when the house was finally silent. The last echo of the children's excited voices had faded away, and Darcy made himself comfortable in a chair in the room that passed for Netherfield's library. A west window admitted the afternoon's sun and more than sufficient light for reading. For a while, the chosen volume held his attention, but soon enough other words and images intruded. Despite his best efforts, Darcy was forced to lay aside the book in favour of a studied inspection of the shelves and their contents. The spines of the books were disturbingly misaligned and not at all ordered by size, but he resisted the temptation to correct that deficiency.

The library at Pemberley was a well-loved and highly valued collection, neatly arranged on shelves behind glass doors, preventing exposure of the more fragile volumes to dust that would further deteriorate the old paper. Darcy took great pride in the selection, the accumulation of which was the work of many generations. A comparison to his present surroundings was not worth considering.

He had seen another library recently, however. The small room at Longbourn where he and Bingley had met with Miss Bennet and Mrs Matthews to discuss the details of their move was quite clearly another example of a well-loved collection. Although there had been no opportunity to peruse the titles, to discover the choices that someone had made in selecting them, Darcy's curiosity had not been extinguished. He wondered who had enjoyed the words contained within the covers. More precisely, he imagined Elizabeth's fine hands fingering the binding in search of her favourite.

It was absurdly simple to envision the lady in such a pursuit. It was less amusing to realise that there might not be another opportunity to see the room or the books in it. Darcy found himself experiencing a sense of injustice that they may be fated to remain with Mr Collins, rather than released to the care of those who had loved them through the years.

Abandoning his chair in frustration, Darcy shook his head at his own folly. These regrets had nothing to do with *books!* It was Elizabeth who inspired his melancholy thoughts—or rather, it was her absence. Elizabeth inspired a different feeling in him.

With that thought came an immediate pleasurable sensation. Closing his eyes, she was before him, an impertinent sparkle in her eyes and a pert lift to her lips. His breath was released in a slow exhale, not quite a sigh, yet a soft moan was impossible to quell as the lady's image continued to tease him.

Reluctantly, he opened his eyes, dispelling the tempting vision. Darcy was not in any doubt of his feelings where Elizabeth was concerned. It had been difficult enough when he had foolishly considered her as a match for his friend, all the while his own admiration was increasing. With that obstacle removed, what was there to prevent him from acknowledging it?

The dilemma lay in reconciling his feelings with his responsibilities. For most of his life, Darcy had considered his responsibilities above his own desires. Many people were dependent upon his actions and choices. Tenants, servants, and now his sister's children would be affected by those decisions.

He was weary of putting aside his own wishes for the welfare of others. It was not that he cared any less, but that after so many years of duty and obligation, he longed for the freedom to be selfish, even for a short time.

It was not easy to throw off the mantle of accountability, thus he stood in Netherfield's library, surrounded by warring doubts and desires, unclear of the direction he should take. His father's words suddenly intruded on his thoughts—words from a long-ago lecture in Pemberley's library. Darcy had been sixteen years old, flush with youthful infatuation.

"Fitzwilliam, I would like a word with you." Waving him into the library, his father closed the door behind them. He was silent for a few moments, studying his son intently. Drawing a breath, he finally spoke.

"Miss Chambers."

"Yes sir?"

Mr Darcy saw the colour rise in his son's cheeks. "She is a pretty young lady. You have been rather attentive to her recently. Perhaps too attentive?"

Fitzwilliam's chin rose, his shoulders drawn back. "I have

Fitzwilliam's chin rose, his shoulders drawn back. "I have done nothing improper, sir."

"I believe you. I did not ask you here to give you a rebuke but to caution you, to refresh your memory of things you already know. The lady's station in society is not such that Miss Chambers should be misled into believing there is hope of an alliance, and she is of too high a position for a mere dalliance. I felt it necessary to speak to you before...enthusiasm overruled your good sense." Again he was silent for a moment, waiting for his son's response.

"Yes sir. I understand." The words came reluctantly.

"I have offended you."

"No sir."

"Son, I know all too well what you are feeling and thinking about the restrictions placed upon us by society. The ladies must also live by these rules. As men, we at least have the greater freedom of choice."

Fitzwilliam's reply this time was immediate. "Choice? With all due respect, Father, it seems we have little choice at all."

The older man shook his head. "Of course there will be disappointment. Do you think I had no tender feelings for any lady before marrying your mother? Or she for another man? We both knew our duty to our families, however, and what was expected of us. As do you. It is a lucky man indeed who finds fortune, status, and love in the woman he marries. You will learn to accept it, as we all have done."

That memory had long been buried, but the lesson was never forgotten. The brief flirtation with a young debutante amounted to nothing, and Darcy returned to his studies. Several years after the death of his father, Darcy dutifully followed his advice.

"Duty!" The word felt gritty as it passed his lips. "I fulfilled that obligation, and what did it bring me? Benefit to Pemberley or the Darcy name as intended? No, I will not go down that road again."

But what road was there? Elizabeth had left Longbourn. Darcy berated his lack of foresight.

Why did I not think to ask more about her home? What if she does not return before we must leave Netherfield?

Almost immediately he was reminded of the fact that the lady was still in mourning. He knew that this was also partly to blame for his unguarded approach. There was safety in addressing a woman who could not, and should not, respond to a gentleman's overtures. There had never been any danger in engaging Elizabeth in conversation, no danger in accompanying her on walks.

Darcy had been free to enjoy the lady's delightful company with the only risk being his own heart. *That* had been entirely unexpected.

Having spent more than twenty years as a bachelor, six years in marriage, and three as a widower, he was astonished by the ease with which Elizabeth Matthews captivated him. There had been his usual resistance, of course. Fully expecting interest in himself and Bingley when they entered the neighbourhood, Darcy was not surprised by the numerous social invitations from those hoping to marry off their eligible daughters. The attempts were mild in comparison to the highly aggressive society to be found in London and quite easily deflected.

Elizabeth was different. She made it clear she had no

designs on either of the single, wealthy gentlemen. Her ease of address, intelligent conversation, and natural humour combined to charm him, without any need for defence.

The notion caused him to smile. *Defence. How would I even consider such a thing?* Just as suddenly he was struck with a shocking realisation. For the first time in his adult life, Darcy knew what it was to need another person. Desire was one thing, but need was a much more potent force. Far greater than simply desiring the company and affections of Elizabeth, he needed her presence in his life.

Darcy slowly began to pace on the carpeted floor of the library, the examination of his feelings continuing unabated.

He had married primarily to satisfy his duty of providing an heir for Pemberley. Unfortunately, that obligation was left unfulfilled. It had not struck him with as much disappointment as it had Helena, however, for he knew Georgiana's son would easily fill that role.

Elizabeth Matthews had rekindled his thoughts of a family. It was not simply the desire for a son but imagining her as his dear wife, bearing their children, that he found so appealing. Now the meaning behind his recent dreams was clear, and he knew she held the missing pieces to complete his happiness.

There remained the question of resolution, however. The situation was not simple. Apart from not even knowing how to find her at the moment, there was the question of the lady's own feelings on the subject. If marriage had taught him anything, it was to take into consideration a woman's opinions when making decisions affecting her.

Impatience gnawed at him. His mind made up, the inability to take action was intolerable. Irritated with himself for being too slow, too indecisive, too much in denial to declare his feelings, Darcy set his thoughts to considering the options available.

The earliest Elizabeth might possibly return to the area was when her mother and sister were settled in their new home. That was a fortnight away. Darcy tapped his fingers impatiently against his leg. The wait would be interminable. It would, however, bring her mourning period that much closer to its end.

Determination would sustain him during that time. Determination and contemplating what to say when they finally did meet again would provide some pleasant distraction in the days ahead.

JUST WHO WAS MORE tired following the trek through Netherfield's lawns was not entirely clear. Anne had to be carried into the house, her legs too weary to take her any farther. Young Charles valiantly fought to stifle a yawn with limited success. Bingley trudged down the length of the hall until he could transfer his daughter into the arms of a servant who took her upstairs, his son following close behind.

Bingley joined his friend in the library. "Mrs Matthews was right. Anne and Charles are exhausted."

Darcy eyed his friend critically. "You appear much the same."

Bingley seemed more relaxed than worn out. "The experience was quite enjoyable. We shall do it again tomorrow and the day after, I have decided." He stretched his legs out before him and sank back into the chair. "You should join us. It would do you good. You look a bit…"

"A bit what?" The words were sharply spoken.

"There, you have proved me right. You are on edge and could use a diversion, plus the exercise will leave you too tired to dwell on those dismal thoughts you always seem to be nurturing."

Rather than taking offence, Darcy smiled. "I do believe you have left behind your own days of nurturing dismal thoughts."

"Yes, and I must thank you for it. The change has brought more peace of mind for me than you can imagine. I wish the same could be said for you, my friend, but you continue to walk the halls at night." Bingley studied his friend for a moment. "Oh, do not look so surprised. If I did not hear you myself, the servants have certainly mentioned it."

"I apologise for disturbing you."

Bingley waved his hand dismissively. "There is no need to apologise! You have helped me to recover from Georgiana's death, and now it is my turn to help you. I must confess that I am at a loss as to how to do that, however. I do not really comprehend what is troubling you."

"It is nothing," said Darcy softly. "I often feel compelled to check on the children during the night, that is all."

"Then you will certainly benefit from accompanying us tomorrow when I take them out. We shall all sleep well at night."

Darcy was not convinced but finally agreed to the plan. After all, it was a more pleasant prospect than spending time with an open book that he would not read. Whether alone or with Bingley, Elizabeth was sure to occupy his thoughts.

CHAPTER 12

IT WAS A RELIEF TO BE BACK IN HER OWN HOME again. The children soon returned to their routine and Elizabeth to her own. The first few days she was busy with correspondence and household matters, leaving no time to regret the company she left behind.

Jane was soon dearly missed, however, and Elizabeth reflected on that first lengthy visit since her father's death.

Mr Bennet's illness had been prolonged, although the end had come suddenly. For too many years, he had ignored the doctor's warnings, and his wife did not have sufficient influence to persuade his compliance. Elizabeth's admonishments went unheeded, and her father succumbed when a trifling cold set in to further test his weakened health.

When the news reached her by express, Jane having immediately penned a note, Elizabeth sat down and cried for a full hour, then made arrangements for her solitary journey home to pay her respects and help Jane comfort their mother.

The quiet at Longbourn that day and in the days that followed was unbearable. Never had Mrs Bennet been driven to silence as she was when the relentless teasing from her husband was no more. Elizabeth spent long nights sitting at his desk, recalling the countless hours she had listened as he read to her from their favourite books. Even before she was able to read, Elizabeth had sought out the comfort to be found sitting by the warm fire while her father's gentle voice wove tales of adventure.

That voice later taught her to laugh at herself and others, to take life as it came, and with a pinch of salt now and again. Such an outlook helped Elizabeth endure those first days without her father's ever-present humour to make light of the solemnity. All too soon, it was time to return home and continue on.

Over the next months, Jane and Elizabeth continued to correspond. The inevitable subject of vacating Longbourn for its new master to assume ownership was a sensitive issue. Mrs Bennet would hear no mention of it, and so her eldest daughter turned to Elizabeth for help. Thus, Elizabeth packed her belongings, and those of her two children, and prepared for a long stay in order to see her mother and sister properly settled. It had been no easy task, and Elizabeth felt affected as she once again entered her childhood home. The lure of her father's library called to her, and shadows of memory lurked in every corner.

She was far from willing to surrender those recollections to a cousin whose only attachment to her home was a point of law!

Somehow she had managed to put aside her indignation and wounded feelings long enough to capture Mrs Bennet's attention. Her mother's cooperation obtained, the matter might have been speedily concluded but for the arrival of a certain gentleman and the age-old distraction of eligibility with a fortune attached.

Elizabeth's initial reaction was amusement, quickly changing to frustration when Mrs Bennet eagerly abandoned the important but unwanted task in favour of her long-preferred habit of finding a husband for her remaining available daughter.

More than once, Elizabeth entreated the heavens, calling upon her father to send a tacit reminder to his wife—a lightning bolt would do! Alas, she was forced to become a tedious and annoying thorn, poking her mother with constant redirection to their pressing need to find another place to live.

Jane was pleasantly distracted by Mr Bingley's frequent visits, Elizabeth noticed. This did not disturb her, for Jane's happiness was long overdue. If it proved a brief sojourn in an otherwise woeful year, it was still well deserved. Oddly enough, Elizabeth was so immersed in contemplating her sister's happiness and redirecting her mother that she paid little attention to her own feelings.

The gentlemen from Netherfield had attracted great interest from more than Mrs Bennet. Two wealthy widowers, still young enough to capture the interest of ladies in their first bloom, received numerous offers of entertainment from many quarters. Disappointed hopes abounded, however, when it was learnt that one gentleman had two very young children and the other quite easily rebuffed advances.

When Elizabeth at last had the pleasure of meeting them, social events being limited due to their mourning, it was with some curiosity that she observed Mr Bingley's tentative conversation and his friend's more detached interaction.

Mr Darcy both annoyed and intrigued her. There were many opportunities to further their acquaintance, each one enticing Elizabeth to delve more deeply in an effort to pierce the man's seemingly impervious exterior. Mr Darcy had proved a delightful target for her humour, and without realising it, she had been drawn away from the fresh pain of grief towards precisely the kind of sport she and her father often enjoyed.

At home again, Elizabeth felt her loss more poignantly. Never had she so strongly wished for a partner with whom she could debate. Her father had always played that role, be it serious or in jest. Elizabeth had not felt the need to cultivate another such relationship, and her selection was certainly limited. Those who remained were guaranteed simply to voice agreement with her opinions or adamantly disagree without a valid argument. There was no interest in debate amongst Elizabeth's acquaintance.

Her last thought gave her pause. There was one person who seemed to be similarly disposed, although discussions with Mr Darcy were quite often more like walking through a pasture. It was always necessary to watch one's step! This only added to her satisfaction in testing him.

Jane's most recent letters had not made mention of either of Netherfield's gentlemen. That did not strike Elizabeth as particularly odd, considering the preoccupation with moving and the addition of Mr Collins and his family. It did leave her with a niggling curiosity, however. There were few of the neighbourhood's residents about whom she would feel inclined to enquire. A reply to Jane was on Elizabeth's list for the day, and so she smiled in anticipation of what she would write.

BINGLEY CONTINUED to cultivate the habit of taking his children out after breakfast through the gardens surrounding Netherfield or in the carriage for a change of scenery. Of course, this did not necessarily have anything to do with the frequent times he encountered Miss Bennet as she walked to and from Meryton. As befitted the manners of a gentleman, he did not once neglect to offer the lady a more expedient means of reaching her destination.

The first time Bingley had the pleasure of taking Miss Bennet home, they spoke politely on neutral subjects, Anne and Charles asking frequent questions about their young friends and when they would see them again. Miss Bennet could only answer that she expected the return of Henry and Cassandra once she and her mother had moved to their new house. This, of course, opened up a floodgate of more questions about the reason for moving, and if there would be enough room for them all to live there.

Both Bingley and Miss Bennet laughed at their curiosity. The complexities of entailment and financial limitation was not something they needed to understand.

On subsequent occasions their conversation grew more casual. With no other adults to overhear, there was no concern for what might be considered undue familiarity between two unmarried people. They learnt more about one another, discovered a similarity in disposition, and a shared interest in the happiness of others. After a while, their conversation naturally turned to the people whose happiness meant most to them.

"I am surprised Mr Darcy has not come with you," Miss Bennet said. "I took him for a man who likes to enjoy the out of doors whenever he can."

"You are quite correct. He does enjoy walking and riding, and does come with me and the children when we explore Netherfield's grounds. When we use the carriage, however, he takes advantage of the quiet house to attend to business letters. At least, he says he is doing that."

"Do you suspect him of some secret romantic correspondence?" Miss Bennet teased him charmingly.

"I would be pleased if that were the reason! Unfortunately, Darcy has laboured under many weighty concerns these past few years. I would like to see him happy once more, but I fear that may not be possible."

She considered this for a moment. "He does not appear to be particularly unhappy, but of course, you are more familiar with him than I."

"That is precisely what I mean," said Bingley, moving a bit closer and lowering his voice to an intimate pitch. "Perhaps it is unwise of me to discuss such matters with you, but you are a kind and compassionate woman, and I believe you can understand my concern."

"Indeed, I can," she whispered. "I often find myself worrying about my sisters, particularly Lizzy. Like Mr Darcy, her loss is permanent, and we cannot force them to forget the pain of their misfortunes. The best we can hope to do is ease the worst of that pain."

Bingley nodded. "Darcy has helped me a great deal. If I could only return that favour and see him finally free of his bitter memories, I would be satisfied."

"It takes longer for some people than for others. Lizzy, I fear, feels the loss of our father strongly. Her husband's death was a devastating blow, but Father was there to help her through the dealings with bankers and solicitors. Lizzy has become far more independent as a result, but she and our father were always very close. I would venture to say that Lizzy was his favourite daughter." She met the gentleman's gaze seriously. "I realise that Mr Darcy's position is very different, but I am sure that time will heal his heart, too."

Bingley's expression appeared remorseful. "I have more than once accused him of being, in a sense, rather heartless. No, no," he quickly said when the lady's eyes opened wide in shock. "He did not take offence, nor did I mean it in quite that way. Darcy has felt it most keenly, both his wife's death and that of his sister. Georgiana was his charge for many years, and he long held a great sense of responsibility for her. I was more selfish in my grief and did not see his until much later."

"He believes he failed her? Is that what he thinks?" Miss Bennet clearly found it difficult to comprehend the degree of pain such thoughts could engender. "That is indeed a terrible burden to carry! But why should he feel so?"

"I believe it because I also struggled with guilt after what happened. I questioned why I went out that day. Could I have prevented the fire had I remained at home?" Bingley sighed and shook his head. "It is all pointless speculation, of course. I can see the same doubts reflected in Darcy. While I was able to let go of my guilt, I do not think Darcy can."

"Oh, but he must! Perhaps you are mistaken about his feelings. It is not so easy to determine these things, and you yourself experienced the same loss at the same time! If Mr Darcy yet believes he might have done something to prevent the tragedy, you must find a way to convince him he is wrong."

"Convince Darcy he is wrong?" Bingley considered the idea and found it amusing. "I can think of many easier tasks."

Patiently, Miss Bennet explained that it could be done very subtly. Mr Bingley's interest in how that might be accomplished made it necessary to plan a trip for the following day, as they were already approaching Longbourn.

Neither of them were disappointed with that idea.

ELIZABETH SETTLED into the comfortable chair next to the window and eagerly unfolded the letter from Jane. She was pleased to read that their mother had suffered no setbacks in her determination to move everything in the two weeks as planned. Great progress was being made in that direction.

With some surprise, she also learnt of her sister's frequent meetings with Mr Bingley. Jane attempted to make it seem a coincidence, but Elizabeth knew better. Two meetings might be coincidence, but each meeting after that was more likely deliberate.

There was but one mention of Mr Darcy, for it appeared he did not accompany his friend on those mornings when Mr Bingley encountered Jane. The gentlemen did not visit Longbourn, of course, and there was far too much to do for Mrs Bennet and her daughter even to visit the Lucases.

Elizabeth read through the letter once, then a second time to make sure she did not miss any details. Everyone was well, for which she was thankful. Mr Collins spent a great deal of time with Sir William Lucas, who showed him the extent of Longbourn's farms and introduced him to the tenants. This effectively kept him out of the way while Mrs Bennet's possessions were being packed and removed.

As she again read Jane's account of the numerous times she had crossed paths with Mr Bingley, Elizabeth was struck by the fact that Jane was going out of doors more often than usual. Was this a result of their mother coordinating repetitions of the event when she learnt of the first from Jane? It was an irritating thought, but Jane's reports held no hint of dissatisfaction in the activity. On the contrary, she seemed pleased by the attention and even hinted that she was beginning to think the gentleman might like her as well.

"And how could he not, dear Jane?" Elizabeth addressed the paper before her. "He would be a fool if he did not."

As for Mr Darcy, the scarcity of his presence only served to reinforce the suspected nature of his friend's outings. He most certainly would not accompany Mr Bingley on such missions. Elizabeth's heart warmed at the thought, and although she had not gained any further information about Mr Darcy, Jane's letter had conveyed some very promising reports that might bring about some unexpected happiness in the near future.

CHAPTER 13

"Lady Catherine!" Mrs Collins was the first to rise upon the entrance of Lady Catherine de Bourgh at Longbourn.

The grande dame took in the surroundings with an air of well-preserved dignity. Stepping very deliberately into the room, she greeted those present and took possession of the most comfortable chair, recently vacated by Mrs Bennet when she politely acknowledged the other woman's presence.

Lady Catherine seemed to be taking stock of the room and its contents, her gaze finally coming to rest on Mrs Bennet. "This must be a most inconvenient sitting room for the evening in summer. The windows are full west."

"I assure you, we never sit here after dinner, my lady."

"My character has ever been celebrated for its sincerity and frankness, and in a cause of such moment as this, I shall certainly not depart from it. A report of a most alarming nature reached me two days ago. I understand my nephew

Darcy has been a frequent visitor to your home. As I was on my way to Matlock, a small detour was no great inconvenience. It is my Christian duty to warn you against encouraging your daughter to seek an alliance with him."

Clearly astonished at first, Mrs Bennet finally found her voice. "I beg your pardon?"

"Mr Collins informed me that there is some expectation that Darcy may form an attachment to Miss Bennet." Lady Catherine brushed a handkerchief beneath her nose and sniffed disdainfully. "Let me be rightly understood. Such a match must never take place. It would be a mistake."

"I took the liberty of informing Lady Catherine of your words to me last week, Cousin," Mr Collins offered. "It was clear that you would not heed my warnings about that gentleman's character."

"Mr Collins has done you an immense service in bringing this situation to my attention," said Lady Catherine. "I am almost the nearest relation Darcy has in the world. There is no one more knowledgeable about his duplicitous nature. You and Miss Bennet will be spared the grief that I suffered and that my own daughter suffered because of my nephew's dishonourable behaviour."

Mrs Bennet gasped. "I would not have thought—"

"No, of course not." The older woman raised her head so that she peered down her nose. "Darcy has every appearance of moral superiority in manners, address, and appearance. His position in society is advantageous. You cannot blame yourself for being deceived." She paused as though to witness the effect of her words.

There were sounds from the front hall, startling Mrs Bennet from her chair. The parlour door opened a moment later, and a servant announced the visitor.

"Mr Darcy, ma'am."

The gentleman bowed politely upon entering the room.

"Please forgive my intrusion, Mrs Bennet, Mrs Collins. I saw a carriage come through Meryton and recognised the crest belonging to my aunt." He turned to face his relation directly. "Lady Catherine, may I request a few moments in private?"

The lady drew herself up straighter in her chair. "I have nothing to say to you that cannot be said here."

"Very well," he conceded easily. "If that is the case, I would not wish to interrupt your discussion." Darcy chose a place and sat down. "Pray continue."

Lady Catherine appeared unintimidated by his presence. "Perhaps you will believe me now, Mrs Bennet. This man whom you have welcomed into your home, *Mr Collins's* home, is the same man who jilted my daughter and is responsible for her death."

"There was never any engagement," Darcy interjected. "Not even an understanding."

His aunt glared at him. "Anne died of a broken heart."

"She died of pneumonia. Anne's poor constitution brought on illnesses of every kind."

"I will not be interrupted! From your infancy it was planned. You were destined for each other by the voice of every member of your respective houses. You refused to obey the claims of duty, honour, and gratitude, and ruined the hopes of my dearest Anne by forsaking her for another!" accused Lady Catherine.

"The wishes were your own," Darcy countered. "They were not Anne's and certainly were not mine."

Mrs Collins quickly rose, pulling her husband's arm and quietly entreating him to go with her. Mrs Bennet was persuaded to leave the room as well.

Darcy and Lady Catherine paid no attention to the others as the door closed behind them.

"Lady Catherine, the only member of our family who opposed my marriage to Helena was you, based on some obscure claim of promises made by my mother before she died." He moved to a chair closer to her. "Anne was never interested in a union with me, nor I with her. You should know, more than anyone, the importance of having a strong and healthy heir to inherit a large, diverse estate. Anne could never have provided one for Pemberley."

"You dare to speak of heirs!" She spat the words. "Just where is yours, I ask? What strong and healthy sons did your wife provide for you? You married that woman on such a pretext, but you see that the good Lord rewarded your betrayal of Anne with a barren wife." Lady Catherine's eyes flashed with angry bitterness. "Then He took her away, along with poor Georgiana, leaving you with *nothing*. It is just what you deserve."

Darcy's mouth set in a hard line. His words were clipped when he spoke. "I see there is still no reasoning with you. I am truly sorry for the pain you feel and for the years that Anne suffered needlessly. However, I bear no responsibility for any of these misfortunes.

"I will not allow you to spread your misguided falsehoods wherever you go, maligning my character and causing disruption to the lives of countless innocent people."

"Do not deceive yourself into a belief that I will ever recede. You ought to know I am not to be trifled with. Nor will I allow another young woman to suffer the misfortunes of my poor Anne. Mrs Bennet will know the truth and ensure her daughter's safety." His aunt braced her hands on the arms of the chair and made to rise.

"It is clear your motivation is not interest in the well-being of Mrs Bennet or her daughter but to punish me for defying your wishes." Darcy got to his feet. "I shall see you to your carriage."

She stepped away from him. "Not so hasty if you please! Obstinate, headstrong, and unrepentant as you are, I am ashamed of you! I shall see myself out, for I need no assistance from you." With a wide sweep of her skirts, Lady Catherine de Bourgh left Longbourn in much the same way she had arrived—resentful and alone.

Standing in the doorway, Darcy watched until the dust from the carriage's departure had settled before he returned to the house. Mrs Collins greeted him with a sympathetic smile and an invitation to stay for tea, though her husband said he would not keep company with such a man and quickly left the room. Mrs Bennet, on the other hand, seemed eager to learn what she was forced to miss earlier.

Mrs Collins handed the gentleman a cup. "Please do not be alarmed by what we may think of Lady Catherine's recitation today. I have heard it many times, and in spite of the fact that I witnessed the events as they occurred, she seems to have forgotten that detail. I was present when Miss de Bourgh contracted pneumonia and sat with her through the long feverish days until she was blessedly released from that pain."

Darcy gave her an appraising look. "I am comforted to know that Anne had the company of a friend during that time. Thank you for your kindness and generosity."

A movement by the other lady in the room drew his eye in her direction. "Please allow me to apologise on behalf of my relation, Mrs Bennet. I understand how distressing her comments might have been for you. I would like to offer reassurance that Miss Bennet is in no danger, no danger at all."

Looking anxious and uncertain of his meaning, Mrs Bennet took a moment before speaking. "I thank you for that, Mr Darcy. It cannot have been easy for you to hear your aunt say such harsh things about you."

• • •

JANE WAS aghast when told of the events she had missed that afternoon. Relieved to have been spared the spectacle, she was nonetheless perplexed by Lady Catherine's motive in coming to Longbourn and imparting such personal details of her daughter's life. Charlotte's insistence that Mr Darcy's account was accurate only made the entire event more confusing. *What had Lady Catherine hoped to achieve?*

A few more judicious questions revealed the one piece of information Jane was lacking: her mother's belief that Mr Darcy had formed an attachment to her. Jane would have laughed at the notion if she had not felt so mortified. It was not the prospect of Mr Darcy wishing to court her that Jane found abhorrent but that Mrs Bennet would have actually voiced such fantastic ideas to others, particularly Mr Collins!

Alone that evening while she readied for bed, Jane considered all that had transpired in the time since Elizabeth and her children left Longbourn. The days had been full at first, seeing to the necessities of moving while attempting to stay out of Mr Collins's way. After meeting Mr Bingley in Meryton, Jane looked forward to leaving the house at the slightest opportunity, on the chance their paths might cross again. Secretly, she was amazed at her boldness. Never before had she considered what her mother would call 'throwing herself into the path of a man'. Mr Bingley was different, however, and that made Jane think differently.

Early on, she had sympathised with his situation and conceded a partiality to the gentleman, although upon reflection, she concluded it was premature to label her feelings in that manner, and only after the recent daily encounters did Jane know the depth of her affection. If the frequency of their meetings was any indication, Mr Bingley's pleasure in her company was equal to her own. Jane felt excitement at the possibility. The challenge would be to keep that excitement to herself and not allow her mother to see it.

. . .

"ARE you going to sit here all night?"

"Hm?" Bingley looked up at his friend who stood in the doorway of Netherfield's library with a curious expression.

"It is late," said Darcy, "yet I find you sitting here staring at the walls."

"I was just thinking." Bingley grinned, abandoned his chair, and crossed to the door. "You are right. It is late." He said goodnight and stepped past his friend and out into the hall.

Darcy continued into the room, returning a book to its place on the shelf. He shook his head at the image of Bingley's foolish grin, knowing the origin from having seen it many times in the past. In Bingley's enthusiasm, he had made no secret of his frequent meetings with Miss Bennet. In the beginning, it had been a friendly association—pleasant conversation and a sympathetic ear for both of them. It was not long before Darcy noticed a change in his friend's demeanour and attributed it to the lady's influence. An additional benefit was that Bingley ceased teasing him about Elizabeth, not that it had made much difference to Darcy's contemplations.

He had been counting the days. It would not be long now before the move was complete, and Elizabeth was sure to come to help her sister and mother settle into a new home. The children would eagerly look for their friends, and Bingley would just as eagerly oblige with invitations to Netherfield. The prospect almost made him grin too, but Darcy checked the impulse.

As quickly as these pleasant thoughts entered his head, so did the recollection of Lady Catherine's visit that morning. He had no idea how her pronouncements would affect the opinions of the Bennet ladies. Mrs Bennet had obviously been shocked with what she heard. Miss Bennet no doubt had been informed by her mother what had transpired in her absence.

How this was going to affect any future interactions between himself and the Bennet family remained to be seen.

Darcy stood for a moment, looking about the room, then extinguished a lamp on the table beside the chair where Bingley had been sitting. The only light now spilled into the room from the hall beyond the open door. Most of the house was silent, save for the distant sounds that indicated servants were performing their last duties before retiring.

In the upper hall outside the bedchambers, he acknowledged the footman tending the lamps, put an ear to the nursery door, and made his way to his room. After his preparations for retiring were done, Darcy dismissed Wilson and sat for some time watching the fire's flames die in the grate. When the last flame disappeared, leaving only orange smouldering embers, he settled into bed and took the book from the bedside table.

Three pages into the book, he laid it down. Not one word had been absorbed. It was pointless to continue the attempt when his mind was elsewhere. Placing a marker between the pages, Darcy abandoned the attempt, put out the lamp, and turned his attention to the effort of falling asleep.

CHAPTER 14

THE DREAM HAD BEEN SO VIVID THAT WAKING WAS a disappointment. If he closed his eyes, Darcy could be with her once again—see her smile, hear her laugh.

Impatience had never been one of his weaknesses, yet it seemed to be his worst enemy of late. Indecision had been rare, too. His innate confidence had always directed him. To be dependent upon another's opinion was something that had not been necessary since before his father's death, and that alone made him apprehensive.

In the course of a day, the entire neighbourhood had heard about Lady Catherine's visit and her accusations. Bingley had returned to report that Mr Collins had seen fit to spread the story in spite of Mrs Bennet's objections and his own wife's warnings. There had not been any concern in the past when Lady Catherine's vitriolic recitals failed to gain a receptive audience. No, there was more at risk this time, and

Darcy knew his every move would be observed with a suspicious eye.

The opinions of the general populace were of less concern than the opinion of one lady in particular, and while her immediate family did not seem to be influenced by Lady Catherine's words, it would not do to ignore the fact that Mr Collins was in need of correction.

ELIZABETH WAS in her sitting room, her hands busily working the needle and thread while her mind focussed on the task. Cassandra appeared beside her chair, and she set aside the mending in favour of her company.

"Mama, when are we going to visit Aunt Jane again?"

"You must remember that Grandmama and Aunt Jane will no longer be living at Longbourn. We must wait until they are settled in their new home. It will not be as large, and we may have to share a room."

The young girl's nose wrinkled in distaste. "With Henry?"

"Yes, even with Henry." Her son was not likely to voice any objections to that. He was usually one to fall asleep as soon as he crawled into bed. "If you would rather stay home, that can be arranged."

That idea was apparently even more objectionable. Cassandra shrugged her shoulders and said that sharing a room with her younger brother would not be so terribly bad after all.

"We shall go into the village to collect the post, and perhaps there will be a letter from Aunt Jane," Elizabeth said. "Please tell Henry to come in so that I can see if he needs to wash before we leave."

Henry was deemed presentable when he appeared, and the three of them set off for the village. It was not a long walk, and while the clouds appeared dark, there was not enough threat of rain to deter Elizabeth from making the trip.

A letter was waiting for her, but it was not from Jane. Elizabeth was surprised to see Charlotte's handwriting. Her curiosity was great, and on the way home while the children explored, she opened the letter to read it.

The contents both shocked and amazed her.

With growing alarm, she learnt her mother mistakenly believed that Mr Darcy intended to court Jane, and she had confided that information to Mr Collins, of all people! Her shock was great upon reading that her cousin conveyed this news to his patroness, and Lady Catherine de Bourgh then paid a call at Longbourn. Her sole purpose, apparently, was to sully the name and character of Mr Darcy!

Elizabeth had to admit that her own opinion of that gentleman in the beginning of their acquaintance had not been glowing. She had since altered that view, and while she was still not entirely sure of her feelings, she could say without a doubt they had never been as poor as his aunt expressed about him. Charlotte's confirmation of Mr Darcy's character being unblemished only served to reinforce Jane's original suggestion that the gentleman was more circumspect than suspect.

Her cousin's behaviour angered Elizabeth. If anyone deserved censure, it was Mr Collins. His latest atrocity could affect Jane's growing friendship with Mr Bingley and not for the good. At the very least, it would cause more gossip and speculation than ever before!

Folding the page, Elizabeth called to Cassandra and Henry to hurry along. She had a letter to write before the end of the day, so it would go out with the next morning's post.

. . .

"DARCY SEEMED to take the news better than I expected when I told him his aunt's opinions are now known throughout Meryton," Bingley said to Jane the next day as he brushed some dirt from Anne's skirt and watched as she ran off to join her brother in his attempts to catch butterflies. "I imagine he is accustomed to Lady Catherine's eccentricity."

"Eccentricity! I might describe my own mother's behaviour as eccentric at times, but from her report of Lady Catherine's visit, the word is far too lenient. I cannot understand how she could say such cruel things about Mr Darcy and how he could tolerate it."

"Disappointment often makes people capable of the unthinkable." They had resumed walking along the sunlit path, and Bingley paused to push aside a branch to allow Jane to pass.

"I was appalled that she would think Mr Darcy had shown any interest in me," she said in a hushed voice, as though the notion was still a secret.

Bingley laughed. "I must confess I find the idea amusing, almost as much as Darcy thinking I was interested in your sister. Of course, both of you ladies are very deserving of attention, but one need only possess an inkling of understanding to realise that those particular pairings are not ideal."

Jane stopped walking and looked at Bingley with confusion in her expression, as though unsure which comment to remark upon first. "What exactly amuses you?"

"Well," he began self-consciously, "some people look only upon the surface. They see two children with no mother and two fatherless children and conclude that the parents would make an ideal couple. Everyone should be happy, yes?"

"Are you saying that is what Mr Darcy thought?"

"Not exactly, but he was under the impression that I might think so." Bingley offered the lady his arm. Jane accepted and they resumed their walk. After a few steps, he spoke again. "I do find Mrs Matthews to be an excellent source of advice on raising children. It is vaguely unsettling, however, to consider that someone else might have thought my interests were of a more personal and serious nature."

"I doubt that anyone but Mr Darcy saw your interest in quite that manner. I am still not sure why that should amuse you."

"Mistaken impressions can result in very entertaining confusion." He turned his head to look at her directly. "I do not wish to appear insensitive, but may I enquire as to the time remaining for your period of mourning?"

The question undoubtedly took her by surprise, and Jane stuttered a response, indicating that another five weeks would see their transition out of formal mourning.

"I apologise if my question caused you some distress. I have long since learnt the value of speaking honestly, rather than assuming others know my intentions." In spite of his brave words, Bingley was apprehensive. "I would like to properly court you when the time is right to do so. That is, if you would welcome my attentions." Once the words were out, he felt a great relief, and his smile confirmed his feelings.

Jane exhaled slowly, and her own smile tentatively appeared. "You will be most welcome, sir."

"Papa! Papa!"

Both Jane and Bingley turned their attention towards Anne to see the little girl jumping up and down excitedly.

"Papa, look! Look!" She pointed to where her brother stood very still, a butterfly clinging to his sleeve. "So pretty!"

Charles proudly lifted his arm to show them his prize, when the insect suddenly fluttered away. His face fell in dismay, but it soon regained animation when Anne squealed with delight as the butterfly landed on her skirt.

"Lovely!" Jane softly exclaimed. She glanced at Bingley to see him watching her with a grin as big as his daughter's.

DARCY REINED in his horse just outside Longbourn's garden gate. Beyond the wall, he could see Mr Collins bent over a small flower bed. Darcy frowned at the sight, wondering what the man could be doing in such a position. Surely, he would leave such menial labour to a gardener!

Dismounting, he tied his horse to a nearby branch of an overhanging oak and strode through the gate. The crunch of his boots on the gravel path brought Mr Collins to an upright position, and he sent a startled look over his shoulder. Upon seeing Darcy, the new master of Longbourn's eyes opened wide, and he scurried away in the opposite direction.

"Mr Collins! A word, sir," called Darcy, quickening his pace.

The other man moved faster, ducking behind a hedgerow. Darcy followed, surprised when he turned the corner to find the next path empty. He stood still for a moment, considering where to go next, then shrugged his shoulders and turned around to proceed to the front entrance of the house. Emerging from the gardens and out to the lawn, he spied the rapidly retreating figure of Mr Collins as he ran across the open space.

Darcy called out again. This time the man did not even look over his shoulder but ran straight to the house and disappeared around the corner. Darcy shook his head and continued on with determination.

The front door was open, and he entered the house, glancing around and listening for an indication of where Mr Collins might have gone. A noise from behind him caused Darcy to quickly turn around, just in time to see his quarry slinking along the wall next to the drive. Darcy calculated the point at which he could intercept Mr Collins and wasted no time getting there.

"Good Lord!" Mr Collins clutched a hand to his chest, brought up short as he nearly collided with the man he had tried to avoid.

Darcy blocked his escape by extending his riding crop to touch the wall behind Mr Collins. "Are you deaf, sir?"

"I do not—" The man swallowed with effort and began again. "I do not know what you mean, Mr Darcy."

"I called your name twice. Did you not hear me?" Darcy's gaze was mercilessly locked on the other man's eyes. "I shall not waste your time or mine. Tell me your purpose in spreading Lady Catherine's falsehoods amongst the local society. You cannot be ignorant of how I would view this. Well, speak up man!"

"Her ladyship's wishes—"

"Are none of your concern," Darcy concluded for him. Lowering the whip, he stepped back to take an appraising look at the man before him. "Collins, you are no longer in my aunt's employ. You are a landowner now, a man of property. You have no need of her good opinion anymore."

The notion seemed new to him, for Mr Collins blinked repeatedly as he considered the idea.

"Come now," continued Darcy, "you were at Rosings the day Lady Catherine sent me from the house with threats of dire consequences unless I relented and bowed to her wishes. You know the true circumstances of my cousin's unfortunate death. Your own wife tended Anne in her final hours." He waited for some sign that his words were having an effect, but the longer he watched the more impatient he felt. "You cannot deny that her version of events is untrue."

"I am not sure—"

Darcy's hand came down swiftly, cracking the small whip

against the stone wall. "For heaven's sake, let go of Lady Catherine's apron strings, and stand on your own two feet!"

Mr Collins flinched at the sound of the whip and again with Darcy's commanding tone. He was compelled to nod, rapidly and eagerly, agreeing as Darcy's instructions continued.

"You will, of course, retract your earlier comments immediately." Mr Collins stood transfixed. At last, annoyed by the silent attention, he asked, "Do you need to write this down to remember? Let us go into the house."

"No, no!" cried Mr Collins in a momentary panic. "I will remember."

Darcy doubted the other man's ability to recall everything he said but decided to alleviate his obvious anxiety. "Very well. Should you forget anything, I shall be more than happy to remind you." He snapped the whip against his palm for emphasis.

Cringing, Mr Collins eyed the whip. "There will be no need," he whispered.

Satisfied, inasmuch as was possible under the circumstances, Darcy warned him, "I realise my aunt possesses an incredible talent for bending others to her will, but be assured the consequences for defying me will be much more severe than any Lady Catherine could inflict. You are a landowner now and responsible for others under your authority. Do not take that responsibility lightly." He dismissed the man with a wave of his hand. As Mr Collins scurried back to the house, Darcy considered his next step.

Daunting as the prospect seemed, he knew that facing the disapproval of the local townspeople would be necessary if he hoped to retain the fragile connexion with Elizabeth and promote a further understanding for the future.

CHAPTER 15

THE MOVE FROM LONGBOURN WAS COMPLETE. There was nothing to do but unpack and assign space for each item as it was once again exposed to daylight. Mrs Bennet directed the maid who had accompanied them to their new home, while Jane gently placed the fragile pieces of china into the cupboards. All of the large furniture had been brought into the appropriate rooms, and once the linens were found, the maid could see to readying the beds before the hour grew too late.

Jane had worried that her mother would be distressed at finally leaving Longbourn, but since the Collinses had arrived, the house had become crowded and noisy. Mrs Bennet had been eager to exchange chaos for the quiet of her new home and had even confessed to excitement in taking the final step to separate herself from her long-time residence. Adding to her excitement was the news that Elizabeth would be joining them by the week's end, and despite the fact that her purpose would be to assist, Mrs Bennet stated her mission was to have as much in place as possible before her daughter and grandchildren appeared on the doorstep.

Jane's mind was also on her sister's impending visit but for another reason. Elizabeth's letters had contained more pressing questions intended for Jane's eyes alone and while their mother was occupied with her happy tasks, Jane was free to contemplate Elizabeth's queries.

It would be impossible to keep the news of Mr Bingley's intentions a secret from Elizabeth, and Jane had no desire to hide her joy from her dearest sister. To share such particulars could only increase her happiness.

The matter of Lady Catherine and her abuse of Mr Darcy was not as easily addressed. Jane had been subjected to several repetitions of the tale from her neighbours, no two quite the same. To each person, she had refuted the story as lies and said that Mr Collins had since realised his error in relating falsehoods. Elizabeth deserved to know the truth, not only about Lady Catherine's accusations, but also how Mr Darcy was troubled by the circumstances of his wife's and sister's deaths. Jane suspected Elizabeth's opinions would be softened by hearing these directly from the gentleman himself.

She looked up at the sound of a wagon passing by the window. The new house was situated closer to the road than was Longbourn, and it would take some getting used to the additional noise during the day. A knock at the door dispelled the notion that it was just a passing wagon, however.

"Jane, this is wonderful!" Mrs Bennet said excitedly as she entered the room. "Four servants have come from Netherfield to help unpack and get our rooms ready for tonight!"

The news was certainly welcome as Mr Collins had only

begrudgingly allowed the use of Longbourn's servants to bring the furniture, and they were under strict instructions to return immediately upon completion of that specific task. The men had been kind enough to risk defying Mr Collins's orders but had reluctantly departed when the hour grew late. The footmen and extra maids from Netherfield would quickly have the house in order and be able to return there before it grew dark.

"How kind of the gentlemen to send extra servants," agreed Jane. "Let us waste no time!"

"THAT WAS QUITE GENEROUS OF YOU," remarked Darcy upon learning that evening of his friend's scheme. "I cannot imagine your next feat."

"Just think about it, Darcy!" Bingley rubbed his hands together. "The maids will return with all sorts of goss—um, observations about the ladies' comfort and—"

"When did you become interested in gossip?"

"And," continued Bingley, as though he had not heard, "perhaps even news of visitors."

Darcy's expression was even more perplexed. "What sort of visitors?"

The other man looked heavenward innocuously. "Oh, I was thinking of young Henry and Cassie. Anne and Charles are eager to see them again."

"I see." In truth, Darcy was not particularly bothered by Bingley's veiled allusions to Elizabeth. It would be convenient to know when she would be expected to return. "You have clearly given thought to this, and I hope it serves you well. The children will be most pleased to resume their acquaintance."

His friend smirked. "I knew you would understand. Now, what say you to a nightcap?"

Darcy agreed, and they sat and enjoyed their brandy in companionable silence, each lost in thought. When the glasses were nearly empty, Bingley suddenly spoke.

"I have asked Miss Bennet for permission to court her in a few weeks when her mourning period ends." He looked to his friend, whose expression did not change, save for a brief flicker of his eyelids. "Have you any objection?"

Darcy started at the question. "Objection? Certainly not. Why should you be concerned that I might object?"

"You are my friend and Georgiana's brother. Surely, you have some opinion on the subject." Bingley waited patiently for a response.

At last Darcy drew in a deep breath and exhaled sharply. "My sister was happy as your wife. You grieved her death appropriately, respectfully, and painfully. Did you think I would ask anything more of you—that I would begrudge you happiness in another match? I never expected you to live the rest of your life without the companionship of a wife, particularly when your marriage to Georgiana had brought both of you such joy. I confess I did not expect this quite so soon, but I cannot argue with your choice of lady. Miss Bennet is not a grasping fortune hunter."

Bingley grimaced. "Really, Darcy! Must you use such terms?"

Shaking his head, Darcy chuckled. "Will you forever be reluctant to accept that such women exist?"

"You cannot believe there are no exceptions."

"I shall admit that there was a time I thought exactly that." Darcy set aside his empty glass and folded his hands. "I was too critical. You were too trusting."

"And now?"

"You have learnt to be wary."

Bingley snorted. "Thank you, but I was not asking about myself. You still appear to me to be too critical at times. It could simply be your choice of words, of course, but the end result is the same."

"How so?"

"Take for instance your words a few moments ago—grasping fortune hunter. Can you not hear the cruel edge in that description? A small effort on your part and you might have said Miss Bennet is a sweet and gentle lady rather than shade the compliment in pessimism."

"Now you seek to provide me with lessons to improve my form of address?" Darcy's questioning expression faded. "Perhaps in years past when my opinions carried more weight with you, I might have attempted to dissuade you from such an alliance for reasons that no longer trouble me to the same degree. You are your own man now, Bingley."

"What reasons do you mean? No, never mind. They are not important." Bingley paused, then added, "It sounds as though you no longer think such details important as they pertain to me, but what about their effect on you? Do the same standards apply?"

"To put it simply, no. I have since discarded my concerns about what certain members of my family may think of the people with whom I choose to associate. The years have afforded me a great number of opportunities to learn the true natures of those who share the same social sphere, and while I shall not condemn them all as grasping fortune hunters, there are many who do fit that description." Darcy's voice became quieter. "I find Miss Bennet reminds me, almost uncomfortably, of my sister, but I did not think it wise to mention that to you. I apologise if you find my words distressing."

Bingley fell silent, mulling over the thought, until he finally said in a quiet voice, "Darcy, may I ask you a personal question?"

"Have we not already delved into personal concerns?"

"Have you given any further thought to my suggestion regarding your own happiness? Surely you must realise that if my plans come to fruition and Miss Bennet consents to marry me, you will inevitably be thrown into Mrs Matthews's company quite often. I still insist that she would suit you very nicely, my friend, if you would but give the notion a chance."

"Bingley, I—"

"Do not tell me that you have no interest in marrying again! What you need is an intelligent companion, and I am sorry to tell you that I will not reside at Pemberley forever. What will you do without my stimulating discourse?"

Darcy left his chair and walked to the doorway as though he meant to leave, then stopped, turning around to face Bingley. "You can have no idea how often that thought has plagued me. I have no wish to see you leave—or Charles and Anne. However, it is your life, and they are your children, not mine. Pemberley will be large and empty, but that is little different than it was not so long ago. You need not be concerned about me, Bingley." He stepped closer to his friend. "I shall only say that your suggestion was not so different from my own ideas. What remains is to see how the lady feels about it."

Bingley sprung from his seat. "Darcy, that—" He recollected the more serious nature of his friend and began again. "I have no doubt of your success."

JANE EAGERLY SOUGHT the soothing comfort of her bed that evening. The day had been long, even with the help of the additional servants, and both Jane and her mother were grateful. So grateful, in fact, that Mrs Bennet insisted on personally thanking the gentlemen responsible for so much of their recent good fortune.

Elizabeth and her children would be arriving within two days. It would be the perfect time to invite Mr Bingley, his children, and Mr Darcy for the afternoon and to stay for dinner. Mrs Bennet was already planning the event, choosing the menu, and calculating the quantities necessary to ensure a sufficient number to satisfy their guests.

By Saturday, when Elizabeth joined them, all was ready. The invitation had been sent to Netherfield and accepted.

"Entertaining already?" a shocked Elizabeth asked upon hearing of the plans. "You have only just moved in!"

"Oh but Lizzy, the gentlemen were so helpful, and if not for the servants they sent to assist us, we would never have been done by now."

"Is this true?" Elizabeth turned to her sister.

"Very much so." Jane gave Elizabeth a look that clearly meant they would discuss more at a later time and without their mother's presence.

"Should I ask if the extra room is made up for us?"

Mrs Bennet quickly answered. "Everything is ready. That was also done while the Netherfield servants were here."

"Come," Jane said, "I shall show you the room, and we can see that the children's things are set out."

She led the way upstairs to the room at the back of the house. It was not large, but it was comfortably furnished, and Elizabeth was pleased to see that the window coverings were drawn back, allowing light to flood the room.

"If you do not mind, Cassie could share my room," Jane offered. "I thought she would not like to share with Henry, and three of you in this room is just too much."

"Cassie would like that, but only as long as you are sure! Do not offer because you feel sorry for her. Cassie is likely to keep you awake half the night with her chatter."

"I shall enjoy her company." Jane sat down on the edge of the bed and glanced towards the open door. Mrs Bennet's voice could be heard in conversation with her grandchildren. "I have something important to tell you."

Elizabeth sat on the bed next to her sister, curling her feet beneath her. "It has to do with Mr Bingley, I assume."

The colour rushed to Jane's cheeks, and she could not hide the smile which appeared. "Oh Lizzy, he wants to court me!"

"I thought he was doing that already. From the accounts in your letters, I understood that you and Mr Bingley were frequently out walking together."

"Yes, but he wishes to formally court me when it is proper to do so. When should I say he may come calling for that purpose? I told him it would be a few weeks yet, but what do you say?"

"I see no reason you should have to wait any longer. Papa would not want you to wait, and you know Mama will certainly agree to the plan." Reaching for her sister's hand, Elizabeth squeezed it reassuringly. "You will not be offending anyone by setting aside the formalities of mourning at this time. It has already been five months since Papa's passing. You will cause no stir by welcoming Mr Bingley's attentions —well, only with Mama, for you know she will not be able to contain her joy!"

"That is precisely why I have not told her anything yet!"

Elizabeth drew her sister close and whispered, "I wonder how long we can keep it that way."

CHAPTER 16

Darcy was prepared for a serious discussion with Elizabeth. In all of their prior exchanges, she had never failed to challenge him. The personal nature of her questions was always offset by the pert manner of her enquiry.

As he dressed for the day's visit, Darcy was not entirely successful in concealing his anticipation. He demonstrated an uncharacteristic indecision when choosing from the clothing laid out for his selection. His mind was elsewhere, working out the many possible directions this meeting might take. Elizabeth had not been present for Lady Catherine's visit, but she no doubt would have heard the rumours circulating about it. Would his intentions be misunderstood or summarily rejected with suspicion? There was no way to discover the answer until they met again. Hopefully Miss Bennet had corrected any misapprehensions which had arisen from the latest gossip.

Inspecting his image in the mirror, he nodded acceptance

of his appearance, satisfied that there was nothing more required.

Mrs Bennet did not intend to disappoint the first dinner guests in her new home. The menu was superb—the repast made from the choicest selections of meats and fresh ingredients.

The children had greeted one another as though they had never been apart. There was not the room previously available at Longbourn, but the weather was fine, so they were able to spend a good portion of the visit out of doors. Over refreshments, the adults conversed on several topics until Mrs Bennet excused herself, claiming the sun was too much for her to bear. This afforded an opportunity for the others to change their seating arrangements to be closer to their choice of partner.

Bingley and Jane were soon engrossed in continuing a discussion that had clearly begun at an earlier time when they were out walking with the children. Elizabeth and Darcy had nothing to contribute, so they sat, each contemplating how to introduce a new subject to their companion.

The four children were busily exploring the garden. It was not a large space, but there was plenty to investigate due to overgrowth, and their discoveries excited their young imaginations. The sight at last inspired Darcy to speak.

"Have you much property attached to your home, Mrs Matthews? I ask because your son seems to be very much enjoying the mysteries to be found in this garden."

"My house is quite modest," she replied. "My husband was a shopkeeper. After his death, my father assisted in the sale of the shop and business so we could remain in our home and receive a steady income to support us." Elizabeth tilted her head slightly, a teasing glint in her eye. "I understand your own residence has some property, sir."

He briefly studied the lady's expression before saying, "It is a large estate, although perhaps not as large as recent speculation might suggest."

"You should pay more attention to your neighbours' conversations. You would be amazed at the things you could learn about yourself." Elizabeth's face was suddenly ashen, and she cast her eyes down. "Forgive me, I did not intend to—"

"There is nothing to forgive," Darcy quietly interrupted. "I have no concern for general opinions, as they are most often based upon superficial knowledge. I do, however, care deeply for the opinions of select individuals." His steady gaze upon her made his meaning quite clear.

Elizabeth drew in a breath, her colour returning. "I have long been familiar with the dangers in accepting such circulated histories as fact. Still, there is often a grain of truth, however distorted it becomes in the retelling."

Darcy frowned in mock dismay. "I believed you to be above the vulgarity of gossip."

He was delighted to hear her laugh. "How short your memory is! It was I who attempted to impress upon you the importance of paying attention to gossip, if not actually believing it."

The gentleman conceded the argument and sought to compose his thoughts. He appreciated that she was patient, for she appeared to be waiting for him to come to a decision rather than continuing to press for a reply. An explanation was deserved, of course, for there was much that had been said and his character had suffered as a consequence.

At last, Darcy began. "At the heart of this matter is the desire of one family member to preside over the wishes of others—namely her daughter, Anne, and myself. Lady

Catherine de Bourgh, my mother's sister, fancied our union would solidify a combined fortune and property that would rival some of the most attractive in the kingdom. She did not anticipate that my strength of will matched her own and that my plans did not include marrying my cousin."

"You defied Lady Catherine."

"Yes, and it did not sit well with her. Anne was of the same mind, but her mother would not listen." He proceeded to relate the lengths to which Lady Catherine had gone in her attempts to persuade him and to discourage the lady he eventually married with threats and dire pronouncements on their future. "Eventually, I was forced to cut all ties with my aunt to preserve some peace in our lives."

"I cannot imagine the selfishness that would drive a person to behave in that manner!" cried Elizabeth. "After all these years, Lady Catherine still harbours deep resentment, too."

"Unfortunately, the tragic circumstances of my wife's death have only reinforced her obsession, convinced as she is that even God has sanctioned her wishes." His lips pressed firmly together with suppressed anger.

"My goodness! It must have been very difficult for Mrs Darcy to contend with such treatment."

"I cannot begin to describe how—" He abruptly stopped speaking and shook his head slowly. "You would not have been affected to the same degree as most ladies, had you been placed in the same situation, I believe. You are an unusually self-possessed and independent woman."

"I fear I am not in the position to argue with you, for I was not there when Lady Catherine de Bourgh graced Long-bourn with her presence. I grant you, however, that I would certainly not be silent while subjected to the kind of lecture I hear was presented. As for being self-possessed and independent, well, I have had many years to practise those qualities —ones my father *encouraged* in me!"

Chuckling softly, Darcy drew the obvious conclusion. "Against your mother's wishes?"

"Against my mother's express objections, of course! Independence of mind and wildness of spirit would never recommend me to prospective husbands, you see."

"Certainly not to most."

Tilting her head to one side, she looked at him with disbelief. "Are you trying to tell me that the late Mrs Darcy was a woman of unconfined nature?"

"I believe I was referring to the fact that you did manage to find a husband who, by all accounts, appreciated your...peculiarities."

Elizabeth's laughter drew the attention of Jane and Mr Bingley. "I have never before heard my nature described in that way. I am not convinced it was my peculiarities that attracted Edward, however. In some ways, I am forced to acknowledge the truth of my mother's words. More than once have I found myself facing disapproval for my unguarded tongue."

"Unguarded? I would say your remarks are occasionally daring but never unguarded. You know exactly what you are about, Mrs Matthews."

As he watched her expectantly, Darcy wondered if she truly realised the effects of her impertinent behaviour. Her father must have been entertained by it, thus encouraging its continuance. He could easily believe Mrs Bennet would be frustrated by her daughter's less ladylike deportment, and he wondered if her late husband had been as captivated as he by her demeanour.

Elizabeth's mouth curved up with a smile. "That is not to say I am always in the right. Would you proclaim that every action you take is unquestionably the correct one?"

"Lizzy, I think you are becoming too serious," Jane softly interjected.

"Not at all," Darcy said in reply to both ladies. "If you find our discussion disturbing, however, I have no objection to discontinuing it.

Bingley leaned towards Jane and loudly whispered, "Darcy enjoys a good argument, and in that regard, I do not provide the best challenge for him."

"Ah!" cried Elizabeth. "You provoke Mr Bingley to argue?"

"I do." Darcy admitted and the others laughed.

That did put an end to further disagreements, and when Mrs Bennet returned to sit in the now shaded garden, the topics of conversation were much less contentious.

ELIZABETH FOUND it impossible to believe that her mother seemed to notice nothing in the looks that passed between Jane and Mr Bingley throughout dinner. There were no embarrassing remarks to urge conversation along, no attempts at finding ways to remove everyone else from the room. Elizabeth knew not what to make of it.

The children ate apart from the adults and under the supervision of Mr Bingley's servants. It was a rare occasion for Elizabeth to enjoy the company of others without the distraction of her children. Observing her sister's enjoyment of Mr Bingley's attention brought great pleasure, but the effort required to parry the comments from Mr Darcy made her feel light headed.

Since the party included young children, dinner was served earlier than usual, and the hour was not late when their guests departed. Elizabeth saw to Cassandra and Henry's preparations for bed, then sent them back down-stairs to bid goodnight to their aunt and grandmother. They were too tired to offer a word of protest.

When Elizabeth at last re-joined her mother and sister downstairs, Mrs Bennet began to question her as soon as she entered the room.

"Now Lizzy, tell me what you think. Mr Darcy does not appear to be the callous rake his aunt professed him to be. Both he and Mr Bingley have been kindness itself during our trying time! Charlotte and Jane have begged me not to believe a word that Lady Catherine said, and now I ask for your opinion. You did hear the story of her visit, did you not?"

Elizabeth sat down and glanced towards Jane to see her reaction. "I did hear of it, and having also heard Mr Darcy's version of the matter, I have to say that the entire affair is quite unfortunate. Lady Catherine's pain must cloud her judgment to say such horrible things about her nephew."

Mrs Bennet's brow creased in thought. "I am still puzzled, however. When Mr Darcy spoke to me the day his aunt visited, he made a point of assuring me that Jane was in no danger, no danger at all. In spite of his words, I have yet to see him declare his honourable intentions towards her."

"I beg your pardon?" Elizabeth's eyes displayed her astonishment.

"It was quite obvious Mr Darcy meant to inform me that he had more serious intentions than a trifling flirtation with our dear Jane."

Elizabeth exchanged a look with her sister, who silently gave her permission to speak openly. "I believe he meant to tell you that he has no intentions at all where Jane is concerned. It is Mr Bingley whose interest is in Jane, not his friend."

Mrs Bennet looked to Jane for confirmation. "Is this true? Has Mr Bingley declared himself?"

"He has, but out of respect for Papa, we shall wait a bit longer to make it publicly known."

"Oh, Jane!" Tears welled up in her mother's eyes, and she quickly dabbed a handkerchief to the corners. "Your father would have been so happy." Overcome with emotion, Mrs Bennet could say no more. She signalled Jane to come closer and hugged her eldest daughter to her in a clingy embrace.

Elizabeth felt her eyes sting and looked away in an effort to stem the flow of tears. When the moment had safely passed, she returned her attention to where her mother now sat smiling, the occasional sniffle muffled by her fine linen handkerchief.

"Now, my Lizzy, what shall we do about you?"

"So, how did you get on?" Bingley tossed a cushion aside and spread himself comfortably on the library sofa. "You seemed to be intent on quizzing Mrs Matthews throughout dinner."

"For the most part, I found her replies odd," said Darcy.

"Do you not think it may have been your questions that were odd?" Bingley laughed. "Or being quizzed at all could have confused her."

Darcy visibly bristled at the suggestion. "My queries were not odd, and there would have been fewer of them had the lady made responses that were more pertinent. Her answers merely led to more questions."

"Down a garden path, no doubt," muttered Bingley, hiding his grin behind a pretended yawn.

"What did you say?"

"Did you at least make your point? Did you discern her feelings?"

"Not entirely." He was silent for a moment, then his expression brightened. "Are you returning to Mrs Bennet's house tomorrow with Anne and Charles for your daily excursion?" At Bingley's nod, Darcy indicated he would be accompanying them. "That will afford me the opportunity to make my intentions clear."

Bingley was not entirely confident the result would be as desirable as his friend anticipated, but he resolved to do his best to ensure Darcy and Elizabeth were given ample time for private discourse.

ELIZABETH WAS STILL TRYING to understand the events of the day, the conclusion of which had her mother redirecting her matchmaking energies away from Jane. That in itself was a good thing. However, the new object of her attention was not at all pleased at the prospect.

Elizabeth had repeatedly, and for several years, insisted that her mother need not be concerned about any future alliances for her widowed daughter, for she was perfectly content as she was. Elizabeth had a small but comfortable home, two children to raise, and sufficient income to see them through.

Mrs Bennet's efforts were frequently more annoying than helpful, although this time, Elizabeth felt more than her usual alarm as her imagination envisioned many embarrassing situations.

She considered the meaning behind Mr Darcy's strange questions and remarks during dinner. On their very first meeting, Elizabeth recalled how interested he was in observing his friend's interactions with Jane. He displayed none of that interest now, yet he seemed inordinately concerned with *her* thoughts on everything from books to the latest news from Europe.

Jane's assertion that Mr Darcy harboured a fondness for her seemed to be reasonable, but Elizabeth was not yet certain about her own feelings. She wondered whether Mr

Darcy was as confused by her replies as she had been by his questions.

The afternoon spent in the garden was pleasant, and Elizabeth had been disappointed when Jane and Mr Bingley interrupted their discussion. She felt the gentleman had been about to reveal something important, and she longed to know what it was.

She knew the routine of Mr Bingley taking his children and Jane out walking was not going to be postponed during Elizabeth's visit, and she wondered if Mr Darcy would be coming, too. That thought immediately made her concerned that her mother would make an embarrassing fuss over that gentleman. With that threat lingering in her thoughts, Elizabeth put her mind to work devising various plans for them to escape Mrs Bennet's notice as much as possible.

CHAPTER 17

THERE WAS A THREAT OF RAIN, BUT IT WOULD NOT deter the gentlemen from making the trip to Mrs Bennet's home. Bingley argued the carriage could hold four adults and four children, even though things might become a bit cramped. Additionally, he knew of a few places where they could stop to stretch their legs, and perhaps his friend would get that much-desired moment of privacy with Elizabeth.

"I think you have done this before," said Darcy as he lifted Anne into the carriage. "Is that how you managed to charm Miss Bennet? Or is it how she managed to secure you so quickly?" The smug expression on his face was not lost on Bingley.

"Save your wit for Mrs Matthews," Bingley advised. "I will wager you will need it today."

Bingley was proved correct in more than one respect when they reached their destination. The ladies were ready and quite prepared to fit everyone inside the compartment.

Darcy's wits were tested as Elizabeth took charge of the arrangements, placing the men on the front seats, so the ladies could face forward during the drive. She sat directly opposite Darcy, allowing him no opportunity to escape her scrutiny. He resisted the urge to shift in his seat and smiled pleasantly in her direction.

"As Mrs Matthews has not yet seen what the area has to offer in the way of sights and walking paths," Bingley said, "shall we ride to one of the more scenic outlooks?"

"Oh, is there a place similar to Oakham Mount?" asked Elizabeth.

"It is not within an easy walking distance, but the view is as pretty, in my opinion," Miss Bennet answered enthusiastically, and Bingley gave the driver directions.

The children filled the time with their chatter, preventing the adults from attempting their own conversations, much to Darcy's relief. Even without knowing the exact answers, Elizabeth easily addressed the questions from her children, as they wanted to know where they were going, how long it would take to get there, and what they would see once they arrived.

Young Henry squirmed in the seat next to Darcy, eventually looking up at the man beside him and saying with a child's boldness, "I would like to sit by the window."

Darcy glanced down at the boy. "Are you asking me a question?"

Henry sucked his lower lip between his teeth and looked to his mother for an answer. She raised an eyebrow expectantly. Turning back to Darcy, he tried again. "May I please sit by the window, sir?"

"You may, indeed." Darcy slid across the seat as Henry eagerly scrambled around his knees and up onto the cushions to peer outside. "But you must sit, young man, and not with your feet on the seat. It is too dangerous not to sit properly in a moving carriage. You might be thrown to the floor if the wheel hits a rut."

Elizabeth offered a grateful smile as her son complied, her expression showing her approval that Darcy had not simply given in to Henry's ill-mannered demand. His correction had been gently done and effective.

It was not long before they reached their destination, and everyone was glad to get out into the cooler air. Anne and Charles had apparently been there before, and they led the way for their friends, showing them where the path emerged from a nearby stand of trees. Elizabeth walked to a barren hillock to survey the view below.

"I daresay it is not as grand as the view from the Peaks, Mr Darcy," she said, "but what do you think?" She did not take her gaze from the scenery, so she did not see that Darcy gave it but a cursory glance.

His gaze was fixed on her. "I have seen nothing lovelier."

Elizabeth turned her head and fell silent. Darcy could feel the flush of colour spreading above his collar.

"Well, I suppose if you prefer trees and pastures to rocks and moss, then this view is admittedly lovely," she murmured at last. "You must tell me more about the country around your home," she said, as though to put him at ease. "Do you have much opportunity to go walking, or do you prefer to ride?"

"Both—I mean, I do both. Pemberley is a rather vast property, and if I do not ride, I take one of the carriages out to look in on tenants." The heat in his face cooled as he relaxed.

"Do you not have a steward for that business?"

"I do, but I prefer to routinely make the rounds of the farms on the estate. It is easier to understand the concerns of the tenants when I can see their conditions first hand." Darcy offered an arm to Elizabeth, and they began walking down the small incline to find the others. "There are many fine gardens around the house as well as a lake nearby and small woodlots that we allow to grow a little wilder. I walk through those daily. It is a source of peace, a calming influence on the mind."

Elizabeth stole a glance at him as they walked. "You must miss that very much, for there is little in the way of fine gardens around Netherfield."

"I miss the familiar surroundings, but cultivated landscape is not necessary for my peace of mind. The exercise does just as well." He lowered his voice to just above a whisper. "I confess that when I am unable to sleep, I take a walk through the house to tire myself, and it usually has the desired effect."

"So it is *you!*" cried Elizabeth. "Lady Lucas once mentioned that someone had been heard walking the halls of Netherfield late at night. She pronounced it to be Mr Bingley and thought that he was in a desperate state of mind."

"Bingley? No, I must lay claim to that habit." Darcy stopped and Elizabeth's momentum brought her around to face him. "Would you object if I were to accompany you on walks while you are here? And perhaps, if it is agreeable, may I call on you at your home once you have returned there?"

"I have no objection, sir." The lady's eyes shone with amusement as she added, "But should you grow tired and wish to sleep, you must find your own accommodations."

Darcy felt his colour rise again at the remark and the direction her daring words sent his thoughts. "I assure you that will not be a concern." He took her arm again, and they continued towards the sounds of the children's voices amid the trees. "Thank you for consenting to my request. It is an honour." Darcy noticed how delightfully her eyes brightened.

There was no need for either of them to say more. Quiet

companionship and the sweet birdsongs soon restored the comfortable ease that had become familiar to him since meeting Elizabeth. It was not long before they came upon the others in a small clearing that opened up to the right of the path.

Anne was perched upon Bingley's shoulders while the boys were leaping up, trying to catch her feet. Cassandra stood off to one side, watching it all with an expression of frustrated impatience and urging them to stop their silly behaviour. Jane merely laughed along with the children.

Keenly aware of Elizabeth's arm entwined around his, Darcy reluctantly relaxed his own and felt Elizabeth's arm slip free. She bestowed a smile on him before moving away to join the children's game, casting an apologetic glance back at him.

"Grandmama says young ladies must be quiet and not run about like wild animals," Cassandra informed Darcy when she noticed him standing beside her. "She says gentlemen do not like ladies who do that."

Darcy bent down slightly to reply. "Very young ladies may enjoy running about just as much as very young gentlemen, and occasionally, even more mature ladies are allowed to enjoy it, too. That will be our secret."

Cassandra stared at him with wide, disbelieving eyes. Darcy nodded reassuringly and brought a finger to his lips, emphasising the importance of the secret. Finally, the young girl smiled and went off to play.

Miss Bennet moved closer, her smile indicating how pleased she was with what she had seen. "Mother has only recently been trying to impress on Cassie the importance of proper decorum. I am afraid she believes Lizzy will allow her daughter to grow up wild and wilful, just as Father permitted her."

"Your sister is not so wilful that she endangers herself or

others. I have had the misfortune of meeting many who do just that, with a wanton disregard for the harm that may result." An amused smile formed on his lips as Darcy observed the antics before them. "No, Mrs Matthews is a breath of fresh air."

"I agree with you, and I would not change Lizzy one bit."

A FEW DAYS LATER, Jane broached the subject of Mr Darcy as she and Elizabeth sat together one evening after everyone else had gone to bed. The gentlemen had come every day, and more than once Mrs Bennet insisted they stay for dinner before making the trip back to Netherfield. The children had a few minor disagreements, as children are wont to do, but it did not disturb the harmony of the adults.

With only another two days before Elizabeth was to return home, Jane felt it time to discover her opinions about a certain gentleman. She hoped her sister would be receptive to his feelings, but Elizabeth was difficult to predict.

"Lizzy, you have not said much about him, but now that you know him better, what are your feelings regarding Mr Darcy?"

Elizabeth chose her words carefully. "He is a most considerate, generous, and thoughtful gentleman."

"He is all that," said Jane with a touch of exasperation, "but that does not answer my question."

"What do you wish me to say? I like him. I like him very much."

"That is a start." Jane sighed. "You know I would not pry, but I think it must be clear, even to you, that Mr Darcy's feelings are stronger than merely liking you. What will happen when you go home?"

"I am aware of his feelings. He asked my permission to visit me at home, and I told him that he may."

This information brought a smile to her sister's face. "I am pleased to hear you are reconsidering your vow never to remarry. You are young with many years to spend in happiness with another husband."

Elizabeth raised her hands as though to put a barrier between them. "I did not say I have changed my mind. Consenting to go for a walk is not consent to marriage!"

"I am sure that is his intent, Lizzy, whatever you prefer to believe. Why would you encourage him if you will not even consider it?" Jane shook her head. "Edward loved you very much, but even he would not have wanted you to remain alone the rest of your life."

Elizabeth threw her head back against the chair, closing her eyes. "I am not languishing in the remembrances of a dead husband like some character from a dreadful novel, believing there could be no other. That would be foolish romanticism!"

Jane blinked as if stung. "Was I mistaken all these years? I thought Edward—that you and he were—"

"You were not mistaken, Jane. Edward was a good man, a very good man. I believe he was happy in our marriage." She paused, as though considering whether or not to say more, then she seemed to come to a decision. "Papa advised me not to marry Edward. Did you know that?"

Jane gasped. "Why? What objection could he have?"

"There was nothing about Edward he found objectionable, but Papa was insistent that I should marry a man who was my equal or my better. He did not feel that Edward reached that mark."

"But you were always Papa's favourite." Jane dismissed the idea. "He would think you too good for any man who asked for your hand."

"I thought the same thing, which is why I did not listen to him. Do not misunderstand, Jane. Edward was the most patient and forgiving of husbands. He loved me dearly, and I loved him. However, he was much more serious minded than I, and often my sense of humour led me into trouble.

"As a shopkeeper, Edward's customers were our livelihood. I could not be myself, and I felt restrained. I know that sounds selfish, but there it is. I never heeded Mama's advice before I married, but afterwards, I needed to put it into practice. I learnt to curb my tongue. I could no longer make sport of my neighbours, for Edward would be offended. I did not want to hurt or discredit him in anyone's eyes, so I changed my ways."

Jane spoke softly. "I never realised—you seemed no different when you were here."

"I could be myself with Papa." Elizabeth's smile was wistful. "And I could not let him see that he was right because it would hurt him, too. When Edward died and the shop was sold, there was no longer any reason for restraint. It was an enormous relief to know that I could once more say what I was thinking in my own house. Jane, I never want to have to lock away my thoughts again. It was like being a prisoner by choice."

"But Mr Darcy admires your outspoken opinions and your impertinent remarks."

"He may admire them now, but will he appreciate such behaviour amongst his friends and family, people accustomed to deference and obedience?" She shook her head. "No, I cannot take that chance."

Jane felt quite differently but recognised that the time was not right to continue the discussion. Instead, she left Elizabeth with something to think about before bidding her goodnight.

"Then you had better be honest with Mr Darcy as soon as possible. It would be too cruel to allow him to believe there is hope after the losses he has suffered already. He deserves better, Lizzy."

JANE WAS GONE before Elizabeth could look up. She saw the door close and was alone to consider all that had been said. There was no point in going up to bed. She would only toss and turn, likely waking Henry with her restlessness.

Jane reminded her that she could be responsible for even more pain inflicted on Mr Darcy, but what about her own? Elizabeth was torn. She did not want to repeat her mistake and spend years silencing herself again. What if Mr Darcy was not as forgiving as Edward had been?

Yet there was another part of her that did not want to give up the exhilaration she felt when in that gentleman's company. His clever replies to her sharp remarks proved that he was the kind of intelligent companion she had always imagined finding.

Elizabeth left her chair to walk about the room. She was frustrated with her own inability to make a decision. It was fear preventing that, she knew. She was afraid to accept the wrong choice again and afraid to reject what might be the right one.

Once more Elizabeth wondered what she had got herself into. She had granted Mr Darcy permission to call upon her, and he had declared it an honour to go walking with her. She had walked out with many a gentleman over the years. Had they all considered it the same compliment as Mr Darcy? She thought not. The implications of his words brought a mixture of apprehension and excitement. Mr Darcy obviously had intentions of courting her, but Elizabeth was not yet sure she was prepared for that.

Still, she had told him he could call upon her! Her heart

had leapt when the gentleman had spoken his request. But was she being too selfish?

She spent some time organising her thoughts, trying to determine how to act. Her children, of course, were her primary concern. There was no doubt that they would benefit tremendously should a union happen with Mr Darcy. However, in spite of their numerous private conversations, Elizabeth still felt she knew too little about the man himself. His past remained a mystery.

It was not that she thought he held any dark or evil secrets, for how could a fine gentleman like Mr Bingley hold him in such high regard if that were true? By all accounts, the late Mrs Darcy had been forced to contend with many hardships, and Elizabeth could not help wondering how her husband may have helped or hindered her.

The answers to her questions were not going to be offered without more prompting, she knew. There was no other choice but to question Mr Darcy directly, as ill-mannered as that might be.

CHAPTER 18

DARCY WAS PERPLEXED BY ELIZABETH'S SOLEMN mood when they walked out the next morning. Her smile and pert manner were absent, thus he decided to make a greater effort to restore them.

"Miss Bennet seems to enjoy entertaining the children." He waited patiently to see if she would reply.

"With four younger sisters, Jane had much practice. Mr Bingley does very well in keeping them amused, too."

"Bingley learnt quickly how to make them laugh. It was helpful in those early days after the fire. Anne, of course, was just an infant, but young Charles needed the distraction." The conversation was not going in the direction Darcy had hoped.

"Fortunately, it is relatively easy to get a child to laugh. The same cannot be said of adults."

Darcy decided to speak more plainly, slowing his pace until they stopped. "What can I do to bring a return of your laughter, Mrs Matthews? You are uncharacteristically serious this morning."

"I am. I should apologise, sir, for it makes for poor company indeed."

"Pray do not be concerned for my pleasure, my dear lady. I am perfectly content to walk with you in silence if it is your preference. I asked on the chance that there was some small way in which I might relieve your mind of a burden."

"I did not intend for my preoccupation to be so readily discernible. I was thinking about my imminent departure and all that it entails. Henry and Cassie will be unhappy to leave their friends."

"And what about you? Will you also feel the loss of companionship? I know that you and your sister are quite close, but surely you have several friends who will welcome your return home."

"I have not cultivated many friendships, but acquaintances do abound. Due to Edward's profession, we knew almost everyone in the area." Elizabeth looked up to address him directly. "And yes, I shall miss the company I have been keeping."

That brought a faint smile to his face as he suggested, "If you have no objection, I could bring my nephew and niece to visit their friends one day when I come." He could see his offer caught the lady by surprise.

"That is most generous of you, sir! I cannot imagine an objection to such a scheme. It will bring pleasure to everyone."

As Darcy hoped, Elizabeth's spirits were lifted. "May I enquire as to your travel arrangements?"

"We leave the day after tomorrow on the afternoon post. That should get us home in time for some dinner before the children must be in bed."

Darcy was shocked. "The post? No, no. I will not permit it."

"I beg your pardon?" Elizabeth's light-hearted tone disappeared.

He realised he had misspoken. "Forgive me, but I will not hear of you going by post when my own carriage is available."

"Oh, but I cannot prevail upon you. There is no need. We are quite accustomed to travelling by post."

"It is no inconvenience, I assure you. I am more than happy to ride alongside as well if you wish, or I could send a manservant if that is what you prefer." He could see her indecision as she considered the choices.

"Thank you. I do appreciate your offer very much. May I let you know tomorrow if I shall be needing the manservant?"

"Of course." He bowed his head politely.

They turned down a familiar path, a shady route lined with wildflowers whose heads waved gently in the breeze. Darcy was reminded of the day he rescued Elizabeth and her children from the rain.

"Tell me, did young Master Henry eventually pick flowers for his mother?"

Elizabeth laughed delightedly. "No, I confess that mission was forgotten soon afterwards. Little boys have short memories."

"How unfortunate."

"Do not say that you will remedy that oversight, sir!"

"Fear not. It is the sole responsibility of very young gentlemen to provide wildflowers. Mature gentlemen must seek out rarer blooms to gift upon their ladies."

Elizabeth steered the conversation in a different direction. "And just what sort of flowers are you known to provide, sir?

Have you a collection of rare specimens lovingly tended in an orangery?"

"As a matter of fact, I do. Of course, the purpose of the building is not only to supply me with exotic flora to impress ladies of discerning taste. It does serve a practical function as well."

Darcy described an enticing environment of fragrant blossoms, brilliantly coloured foliage, and sweet, tender fruits. Expert care and maintenance assured that quality and sufficient quantity were met.

"Your descriptions are so vivid! I can easily imagine myself amongst the blooms and can even smell them right now!" cried Elizabeth. "I have been fortunate to visit an orangery long ago on a trip with my aunt and uncle. But you, sir, had the privilege to enjoy it your entire life! How delightful that must have been!"

Darcy shook his head. "The orangery itself was constructed before I was born, but my father had only begun to fill it before my mother died. He then lost interest in further improvements. When my sister grew older, she became curious about it and encouraged me to expand the variety of plants found there. However, it was my wife who arranged to bring some of the more rare items from her father's estate. She even managed to persuade him to give up one of his highly prized gardeners to oversee Pemberley's orangery."

"Well, she certainly had some influence over her father." With a look of innocence, Elizabeth asked, "Did her powers extend to influencing her husband, too?"

Darcy replied in a measured tone. "They did insofar as a wife generally influences her husband."

He did not look away, encouraging her to speak, but she seemed to struggle for a response until Darcy at last spared her the effort.

"I imagine your husband relied upon your talents to increase the success of his business. Did your smiles and conversation charm the local populace into purchases they may not have intended when entering the shop?"

Elizabeth laughed. "Oh my! I cannot say if I had that effect. It was certainly not by design, but perhaps there is some truth in it."

"Of that I am certain. Your husband was a fortunate man."

Elizabeth blushed under his gaze, and her next remark was obviously intended to distract him.

"If I understood correctly, your aunt is also a persuasive woman."

"That depends entirely on the person she wishes to persuade." Darcy frowned slightly. "For example, Mr Collins is a perfectly willing supplicant for her efforts. I am not. Her methods, I must add, hardly qualify as charming."

"I would never have known from my cousin's lavish praise of Lady Catherine. He has never spoken an ill word of her. Unfortunately, I have only the opinions of others by which to judge her, having never made her acquaintance."

"There are many who would consider that extremely fortunate."

"Including you," Elizabeth sweetly concluded.

"As you know, I have disagreed with my aunt and incurred her wrath. I do not take lightly such interference in my affairs, and her continued abuse of my wife extinguished the last of my respect for her." Attempting to lighten the conversation, he added, "It is a pity we cannot choose our relations."

"Indeed. I have Mr Collins!"

There followed a period of silence while they walked. The ground became uneven, requiring Elizabeth to accept his arm. Through the trees to the right, they began to see open fields. Soon, they would come to the end of the path and be forced to go back.

Elizabeth suddenly turned to Darcy and asked, "Would you mind if we stop for a few minutes up ahead?"

"Are you feeling tired?" he asked with concern. "We have come a long way."

"No, no. I am not tired at all. I thought it would be pleasant to stop for a while, and there is no hurry to return."

"I see. Very well," he cheerfully responded. "As you wish."

At the end of the path was a small area cleared of trees and brush. The way was blocked by a stone wall that encircled a large pasture. Several cows gazed impassively at them before returning to graze. Elizabeth leaned against the wall, Darcy taking up a position at her side. He stood tall and straight.

"Would this be an example of my charms being used to persuade you, Mr Darcy?"

"No persuasion is necessary where there is no objection raised."

Elizabeth pursed her lips in thought. "Well, you have effectively argued away the persuasion, but what of my charms, sir?"

"Your charms are as undeniable as ever." Darcy gave a low bow, taking Elizabeth's hand in his and pressing his lips to it. Just as quickly her hand was released and he stood, still and silent as before.

Elizabeth exhaled softly. "You, sir, have a charmingly frustrating manner of avoiding answers."

He was genuinely surprised by her comment. "It is not intentional, I assure you."

"To what do you refer? Avoiding the answer or being charming?"

"Both," replied Darcy with a small smile.

"You would have me believe it a natural consequence of your charm."

"I make no claim of any kind, my dear lady. Whether my manners are charming is not for me to say. You would not be the first, however, to label them frustrating."

"Pray tell, how many others have informed you of this?"

"Most notably Lady Catherine, who certainly does not consider me charming. Bingley, my sister, and my cousin number among the many. There was also my father, who was probably the first to inform me that my stubbornness was not at all charming." He waited for Elizabeth's laughter to subside before offering an excuse. "I was much younger then, and I sincerely hope I have improved in the intervening years."

"What of your wife, Mr Darcy? I know so little about her. Did she find you frustrating, or did your charms persuade her otherwise?"

"I thought by now we had established that I profess to possess no charms, Mrs Matthews."

"There you have it," she countered. "Yet another example of you avoiding an answer to my question."

"Let me rephrase, if you please. As I have denied possessing any of the aforementioned charms, it must thereby follow that what remains is frustration. There is ample support for its existence. Therefore, I must conclude that my late wife did find me a frustrating companion."

"Perhaps it is the question that needs rephrasing. Did your wife excuse your stubbornness because she liked you, or did she prefer to argue instead?" Elizabeth concluded with a triumphant look.

Darcy spoke slowly as he searched his memory for proof. "I would like to say I gave no cause for such a reaction, but that would be deluding myself," he said with a steady eye on Elizabeth, "and you would surely not believe it."

"Quite correct."

"However, you did not offer much choice in my selection of reply. Either my wife preferred to argue, or she excused my behaviour. Where is the middle ground? What if I were to tell you that we conversed intelligently and civilly when in disagreement?"

"Ah, but we were not speaking of disagreements. The situation put to you was one of your stubbornness." Elizabeth leaned one elbow on the stone wall, her eyes bright with the excitement of a challenge.

"Perhaps a practical test." Darcy settled himself against the wall as well, facing her squarely. "We might continue to disagree, to which I shall stubbornly refuse to give way, and we shall see how I fare at the end."

"There is one flaw in your plan, sir. I will not necessarily react in the same way, for I am not your wife."

Darcy blinked. "No, of course," he said in a subdued voice. "You are not my wife."

Elizabeth stepped away from the wall and was completely oblivious to the way the gentleman's eyes followed her every move.

Her laughter was light as she called over her shoulder, "I am still no closer to an answer than I was before, but it is time we started back. Perhaps you will think of one on the way."

Darcy doubted that possibility, for his mind was far too occupied with admiration for the lovely, impudent lady ahead of him on the path.

Elizabeth waited for him to join her, then set a brisk pace in keeping with her elevated spirits. She was not finished with her questions. "How long were you married?"

"Six years," Darcy said, relieved that this answer was simple enough, for his mind was beginning to feel unusually muddled.

"Six years?" Elizabeth repeated with undisguised astonishment.

Darcy noted her reaction. "You had formed a different opinion? I assure you that six years is correct."

"I do not question the accuracy of your memory. I did think it to be less, but that is not important. I was merely curious." With a sidelong glance at him, she said, "How else am I to learn more about you unless I ask?"

"That is the best method, I agree," he replied, "although the accuracy of the information could vary depending on the source."

"I promise I shall not ask Mr Collins or Lady Catherine but confine my queries to the most unimpeachable source —yourself."

"I thank you," said Darcy with a tilt of his head.

The walk back did not seem as long. They were already nearing the end of the path, approaching the place where it joined the main track, when Elizabeth's foot slid into a hole, and had she not righted herself, it would have been an easy thing for Darcy to catch her, to take her in his arms. He could almost feel the weight of her now, pressing against him as if he held her to his chest. He shook his head to dispel the sensation, the motion catching Elizabeth's notice.

She looked at him curiously. "Are you well, Mr Darcy?"

He could have said he was. He *should* have said he was. Instead, Darcy once more shook his head, and she stepped closer, the expression on her face changing from puzzlement to concern.

"Mr Darcy?" she said again, one hand reaching out to touch his shoulder.

Darcy caught her hand, gently drawing Elizabeth towards him. She did not resist. Rather, her body relaxed as his other arm encircled her waist. A delightful blush crept into her cheeks, tracing a crimson hue along her neck and up to the tips of her ears.

There was no second thought as Darcy brought his lips to her burning cheek. In another moment, his mouth brushed hers ever so softly, while he pulled her body closer.

It seemed like a moment, or a lifetime, until Darcy slowly released his hold, and Elizabeth sank against him.

He lowered his head so that his whispered words reached her ears. "Forgive my presumption, Elizabeth." One finger traced along the edge of her jaw.

With a jerk, Elizabeth's palms pushed against his chest until she was able to gain some distance from him. Her voice was breathless as she said, "Is that how you would describe your actions, sir? I did not think I had given you any cause to believe I had invited you to kiss me. If you think my widowed status grants you greater licence, allow me to correct you!"

She gave him no time to respond, pushing back her shoulders as she continued. "I shall not presume to know the nature of the understanding that existed between you and the late Mrs Darcy, but my own husband and I shared a respect for one another that I will not allow you to compromise!"

Spinning abruptly on her heel, Elizabeth began to walk away, but Darcy's hand was immediately on her elbow. He stepped around to face her, his cheeks as red as though he had been slapped.

"I ask forgiveness for my impetuous behaviour, Mrs Matthews, and I ask that you also forgive my foolishness." His voice was even, yet edged with something akin to regret, lending credence to his words. "I had no intention of compromising your morals in any way, and I am heartily sorry that you should be led to believe so." His fingers released her arm as Darcy turned his head to look away. His hand dropped to his side. "I was not aware that the failure to speak of my wife carried such weight in your opinion. It is precisely because of the respect I held for my wife that I do not speak of her."

As he paused to draw a breath, Elizabeth said, "Perhaps we do not agree on the meaning of respect, sir."

He drew his shoulders straight. "I believe, madam, that there is a tendency for some people to confuse respect with the more intimate emotion of love." His eyes held hers for a tense moment until Elizabeth's chin came up in challenge.

"If by that you mean to imply that I do not understand the difference—"

"Had I wished to imply anything, it would have been the respect I have for you." He hoped the gentle tone in his words would at least convey the depth of his regret.

"Your actions speak to the contrary."

He had no choice but to agree, lowering his head in acknowledgement. "I fear my actions have confirmed Lady Catherine's words. I can only once again ask your forgiveness. Obviously, I was mistaken in my estimation of your regard."

Darcy bowed quickly, and after a moment of tense silence, they began to walk again.

"What exactly did you mean by the words, your estimation of my regard?" She did not look at him directly but clearly expected a reply.

Darcy felt the heat of embarrassment rise again, but this time he knew it was truly earned. "In the short time we have been at Netherfield, I have observed that the townspeople gauge the relationship between a husband and wife by what the surviving partner reveals about the departed," he answered in a soft voice. "This has not necessarily been my experience. Perhaps you have not, amongst your acquaintance, met those who lament the loss of a husband or wife who when alive was more often eschewed than praised. Upon the death of such a person, their virtues may often be elevated in the memories of the loved ones left behind."

Elizabeth did not contradict this observation.

"I do not subscribe to this practice," continued Darcy. "Yet, I must caution you not to mistake my use of the word respect to denote an absence of feeling. Just as you harboured tender affection for Mr Matthews, I am sure, pray do not consider my reluctance to speak of my wife as proof of any ill regard.

"I fear I mistook your persistent questions for interest in me, Mrs Matthews," he continued. "I should have known better." With these words he stopped walking and stood silently.

Elizabeth remarked that they had reached the outer edges of the wild gardens surrounding her mother's house. "Oh! I cannot face my mother at the moment. I need time to compose myself."

Darcy observed the distress in her voice and in her countenance. A grimace formed on his own face and then quickly disappeared. He wrapped her arm around his, firmly saying, "This direction looks inviting. I believe we have more to discuss."

Elizabeth made no objection as they moved away from the house and towards the open lane.

CHAPTER 19

THEY WALKED WITHOUT SPEAKING UNTIL THE house was no longer in sight. Mr Darcy could not have voiced her thoughts any more accurately, and Elizabeth was suddenly ashamed she had not paid more heed to Jane's cautionary words from the beginning.

As the distance from the house grew, Elizabeth's apprehension of a repetition of his earlier conduct was lessened. The road was much more public than the one they had left.

Mr Darcy seemed to sense the lady's tension waning and after a moment said, "May I speak plainly?"

"Please do."

"I believed I had made my intentions known to you, but in the event that it was not clear, I shall now attempt to make it so." He drew in a breath and began. "I arrived at Netherfield with no thoughts at all of meeting a lady such as yourself. Neither was I interested in pursuing the acquaintance of any lady for more than was necessary for general company.

However, I was caught unawares, and you captivated me almost from the first moment of our meeting."

Elizabeth stole a glance at him as he spoke. Studying his face, she was beginning to comprehend the depth of feeling that his words could not convey.

"I am a private man. I do not like my life's details made widely known. Lady Catherine has, much to my dismay, necessitated relating many unhappy details that should never have been made public." Darcy's fingers closed gently on Elizabeth's arm, and she sensed the strength of his emotions. "When my aunt brought her distorted tales to Longbourn, I was more concerned with the effect her words would have on you and your family than any effect they would have on me." His eyes searched hers for understanding. "I knew at that moment that my heart was yours, Elizabeth, regardless of what little hope there was for your acceptance."

She inhaled sharply, and her pulse quickened.

"When you discounted Lady Catherine's claims, it instilled in me a hope of eventually winning your hand." Darcy halted in the roadway, bringing Elizabeth around to face him and taking hold of both her hands in his own. "What do I need to tell you? You have been asking many questions, plainly unsatisfied with my answers. What exactly do you wish to know?"

Elizabeth was still stunned by his earlier revelation and was not entirely sure how to say what had been occupying her mind. "Everything. I feel I hardly know you at all, while I have freely offered many details of my own life."

"I am unaccustomed to revealing intimate information about myself. Usually, there is interest only in that which is already widely known, such as my estate and fortune. To ask personal questions or engage in lively debate has never been attempted by anyone other than my relations or close friends such as Bingley." With a wistful smile he added, "And you."

"And Mrs Darcy?" she asked. "Do you realise that not once have you referred to her by name?"

He spoke softly. "Her name was Helena."

Elizabeth acknowledged this information with a tentative smile. "Tell me more about Helena."

He lifted his head, and he looked away, over Elizabeth's head into the distance. "Where shall I begin?" he asked, more to himself than to her.

They walked again, his history unfolding slowly. Elizabeth listened intently, absorbing every detail.

"Helena was...unremarkable in most respects. She was young and pretty—in her second Season when we met—the only daughter of a wealthy family. Her mother had died a few years earlier. Unassuming and quiet, her temperament seemed to match my own. We conversed on many subjects, never having a serious disagreement, although Helena's opinions did sometimes differ from mine."

Elizabeth thought of her persistence in provoking him and considered that perhaps she was more stubborn than she would care to admit.

"Her family approved of my suit and our courtship was brief. My family, with the exception of Lady Catherine, supported my choice. My sister was overjoyed to finally welcome another woman into our home. Pemberley felt less empty. Helena and Georgiana quickly became as close as true sisters.

"Within three years of our marriage, Bingley asked for Georgiana's hand. I could not have been more pleased. Helena guided my sister through the planning and preparations to a very successful wedding celebration. Before another year was out, Georgiana and Bingley were blessed with a son. Charles was strong and healthy, and my sister quickly recovered her good health."

Darcy paused for a moment. Elizabeth noticed that his

expression altered as though he were steeling himself for what was to come.

"Our lives changed from that point onward. Helena's greatest desire was to have a child, yet that blessing eluded us. Seeing Georgiana and her baby—the joy that motherhood had brought to her—served as a painful reminder of what Helena was denied. Jealousy eventually took root.

"I will confess to experiencing disappointment in our childless state, for it is important that a man of property has an heir. It would be foolish to deny that it was not a factor in my decision to marry. After four years, however, the hope for a child was fading. In the absence of any direct heir of mine, Pemberley would pass to Georgiana and then to her son.

"Perhaps my acceptance of this contributed to Helena's growing bitterness. We had weathered Lady Catherine's continual harassment until I put an end to all contact with my aunt, but I believe that Helena may have viewed my resignation to the fact that I would never become a father as a final act of betrayal.

"Our relationship became strained. With the birth of Georgiana's second child, the situation with Helena grew intolerable. It was increasingly difficult to leave her for extended periods on her own. She had become focussed on that one desire to the exclusion of all else." Darcy briefly lapsed into silence.

"I can only sympathise with her position. Without children, a marriage must be a vastly different experience."

"I know of many couples who live happily together without children. I would have been content with such a fate, but for Helena it was impossible. She would not accept my assurances. I could do nothing to ease her mind." Once again he fell silent, and when he next spoke, his tone was distant, detached.

"She had always been somewhat careless and forgetful,

but that became worse due to her preoccupation. Her maid would frequently find the bedside candle had burnt out by morning because Helena had not extinguished it. Plates, cups, and glasses left too close to a table's edge would fall and shatter on the floor. More than once a servant would stamp out a fire from a lamp that had fallen."

Elizabeth's sharp intake of breath brought his eyes to meet hers. "You think the fire..." She did not complete the thought aloud.

"I do not know for certain, but yes, the possibility has never been far from my thoughts. Did Helena unintentionally cause the fire that killed her and Georgiana? Perhaps. Helena, at least, was no longer tormented by her jealousy." Sighing heavily, he looked away again.

"Of course I was angry, furious with Helena for the carelessness that finally claimed not only her life but that of my dear sister. My nephew and niece were suddenly motherless." He closed his eyes as though in pain and added in a voice so quiet it was almost a whisper, "I even wondered if the fire had been deliberately set."

"No!" Elizabeth gasped.

Darcy nodded sadly. "I discarded the notion quickly, once my anger receded and my head cleared enough to think more rationally. Helena's jealousy had been great but not to the point of violence. She never wished Georgiana harm."

"And you have kept this to yourself all these years!" Elizabeth imagined the weight of the guilt he must have experienced.

"I have told no one until now. It would do no one any good to speak of my suspicions. That could only add pain to an already grieving Bingley and cast a shadow on my wife's memory. What would be the point?"

Elizabeth was forced to agree, but she now realised how much it must have haunted him over the years. "As terrible as it was, the fire was simply a horrible accident," Elizabeth said, reaching out her hand to rest on his. "That is what you must remember."

Darcy looked down at her hand, then turned his palm up to close his fingers around Elizabeth's. Neither said a word, but their pace slowed as they resumed walking and Darcy's shoulders relaxed.

Elizabeth thought about all he had said. "I wonder that you came to be attracted to me. I am not at all like your late wife. I am not unassuming. I have strong opinions, and I let them be known. If I disagree with you, it will not be a secret. I fear your family might be less inclined to approve of me."

Darcy merely smiled. "The members of my family whose opinions interest me will be as taken with you as I am."

Elizabeth, feeling he had not listened to anything she had said, firmly insisted, "I will argue with you when we disagree."

"Then you will obviously have reason to do so," he replied unperturbed.

"I can also be very stubborn," she added in a final attempt to make him understand.

"That is one of your charms, my dear Elizabeth."

She had no answer to that and laughed at his cleverness. Darcy maintained a singular focus on the road ahead.

MRS BENNET PEERED out the window overlooking the garden. "Do you think they lost their way? Lizzy is unfamiliar with the area."

Putting aside her needlework, Jane said, "Do not worry so. I am sure they are only enjoying the fine weather."

"They have been gone so long." Her mother was still at the window. "I thought they were coming in when they first returned, but when I looked again, they were nowhere to be seen!" She turned towards her daughter. "You must go search for them."

"Do be serious. They are not lost. Lizzy has walked the paths here often enough already, and I am sure Mr Darcy knows his way as well. They will be here before long."

Mrs Bennet scurried from her station to take the chair next to Jane. "Oh, perhaps he has proposed!" She sighed and dropped her hands into her lap. "No, Lizzy has done nothing to encourage him. What is wrong with that girl? She spends hours walking with him every day, yet makes no progress at all! She still has a shapely figure in spite of having borne two children, but does she use that to her advantage? No, she simply will not listen to my advice. Jane, you must tell her to work harder. Mr Darcy is not going to wait for her forever, and I heard in the village that several young ladies have noticed his presence. If Lizzy does not secure him, then one of them certainly will!"

"Mama, please!" Jane cautioned with a glance towards the other end of the room. "The children will hear you."

Her mother merely shrugged her shoulders. "Well, I shall ring for tea. At least it will be ready when they finally arrive." Before she could rise, however, the sound of the front door was heard, and in another moment, Elizabeth walked into the room.

"Mama! Mama!" cried Cassandra and Henry, running to her. Elizabeth knelt down and hugged them both at once.

"Grandmama was worried you were lost," Cassandra dramatically announced.

"Is that so?" Elizabeth looked at her mother.

Mrs Bennet's mind was elsewhere, however. "Where is Mr Darcy?" She peered around the open door into the hall. "Is he not coming in?"

"Mr Darcy stayed longer than he intended and has left for Netherfield. He assured me he will return tomorrow with Mr Bingley. And," she said to her children, "your friends."

That news merely served to send Mrs Bennet into another spasm of delight and the children squealing with excitement. The distraction was enough that Elizabeth was spared further questioning, and by the time calm settled once more, only Jane continued to cast curious glances in her sister's direction.

DARCY'S THOUGHTS occupied him on the ride back to Netherfield. He berated himself for his blind stupidity and his impulsive, uncharacteristic behaviour. It could have all gone so wrong.

"I did not think I had given you any cause to believe I invited you to kiss me, Mr Darcy," she said.

"Not to kiss you, no, but how could I resist, Elizabeth?"

A moment of weakness, her expression of concern, and he was lost. Remembering the warmth of her lips, the softness of her body in his arms, Darcy was nearly toppled to the road as his horse suddenly shifted beneath him.

Regaining his seat, he kept his attention focussed on the ride to avoid another potential spill. It would not do to break his neck, not when he had every reason to look forward to the future!

Young Charles and Anne were the first to see him approach the house when Darcy arrived at Netherfield. They both ran to him in excitement, Anne wrapping her chubby arms around his knee. The boy demonstrated more restraint, even though he was unable to stand still.

"Uncle, we are going to take our friends for a ride in the

carriage tomorrow!" Charles proudly announced. "Papa says we have been very good today."

Lifting Anne up to carry her, Darcy smiled at his nephew. "I am pleased to hear it. They will be returning to their own home in two days, so you must be sure to enjoy the time you spend with them."

"So soon?" Bingley emerged from a nearby room with a letter in hand. His expression was silently enquiring.

"Yes, and if you two continue to behave, I may take you for a visit to Cassandra and Henry's home next week," Darcy said with a glance at his friend. He saw Bingley's smile widen with the realisation that Mrs Matthews's approval for that plan had already been obtained. "Now, I need to change from these dusty clothes. What were you doing before I returned?" he asked of Anne.

She wrinkled her nose. "Lessons."

"Did you finish them?" Darcy asked.

Charles shook his head.

"Back to work, then," said their father. Darcy set Anne down, she took her brother's hand, and he led them up the stairs to their governess.

Bingley looked at his friend and said, "I need to speak to you."

"Can it wait until I have washed and changed? The road was dusty."

"It will not take long."

Darcy inclined his head towards the study and followed Bingley.

"I need to reopen Larkston Manor," said Bingley when the door was closed behind them.

"Your house?" Darcy shook his head. "Are you planning on leaving Netherfield?"

"No, well not immediately. I mean—" He stopped, gathered his thoughts, and began again. "I would not feel right about making an offer to Miss Bennet until I face what I have avoided all this time. I realise you saw to its repair and restoration, but there are other personal aspects that must be put away or changed before I can bring a new wife there. Do you understand?"

Darcy had to admit that he had never considered the matter in that respect. Hearing his friend put it in those terms, however, made perfect sense, and he thought about what alterations might be needed at Pemberley, too.

"Do you not think Miss Bennet might want to be involved in these changes? She will be living there after all. It should reflect her taste, or are you not convinced she will accept you?"

"There is always room for some doubt, of course, but I had not considered consulting her before making arrangements for redecorating. Thank you for suggesting it."

He was silent long enough that Darcy asked, "Is there anything else before I go?"

"Yes." Bingley waited for his friend's full attention, then said, "Should I presume that you have come to an understanding with Mrs Matthews? You were away longer than usual today, and from your remark to Charles, I concluded that she has granted you permission to call at her home."

Darcy looked down at his feet. "I concede that taking the children to visit serves a dual purpose, but it was not necessary to make the offer, as I was granted the privilege prior to suggesting it."

Bingley chuckled. "I say, who would have thought when we left Pemberley that both of us might be engaged before the year was out!"

Darcy could only shake his head, amused at the way Bingley could simplify even the most complex circumstances.

CHAPTER 20

"THE CHILDREN ARE ALREADY ASLEEP. COME INTO the sitting room. We need to talk, Lizzy." Jane's tone indicated she would not allow anything but compliance.

Elizabeth knew perfectly well what the topic of discussion would be and had prepared for it in the hours since returning from her walk with Mr Darcy.

"Sit down," Jane directed, taking a seat on a chair near the door. Once Elizabeth was settled, she asked, "What happened today? Mama saw you and Mr Darcy near the garden, and then you were gone again for another hour or more. You did not tell him how you feel about marriage, did you?"

The answer was simple. "He kissed me. You must be shocked," said Elizabeth. "I was, too."

"No, I cannot say I am shocked. I did warn you that he wanted to court you. A kiss might be forward but not surprising."

Elizabeth eyed her sister closely. "Has Mr Bingley kissed you?"

A rosy colour tinted her cheeks. "Yes, he has."

"I do not mean a kiss on the hand or a peck on the cheek, Jane. I mean has he kissed you as a man in love kisses a woman. That is how Mr Darcy kissed me." Ignoring Jane's astonished expression, she continued. "We walked farther because there was much more to be discussed between us."

"You must have been very angry with him! I cannot believe he would behave so badly. Oh, how could I have been so wrong?"

Elizabeth found it difficult not to laugh. "Do not distress yourself! It just happened, and although I was angry at first, Mr Darcy promptly apologised. I did say some hurtful things, but it is all forgiven now."

"I do not understand." Jane took Elizabeth's hands and held them tightly. "Tell me what you mean. Last night you were firmly set against forming any attachment, and now you appear to embrace the idea. Do not tell me it was because Mr Darcy kissed you. I will not believe that!"

Her sister shook her head. "No, we spoke at length, and Mr Darcy put my mind at ease. You scolded me for being suspicious because he did not speak of his late wife. You were so right when you told me he might be too affected by the circumstances of her death." Elizabeth lowered her head and peered up at Jane like an admonished child. "I feel very foolish for everything I said."

"What about the other reasons? Are you satisfied his feelings will remain constant?"

"I listed my less temperate qualities for him. He was not frightened. Rather, he provoked me instead, the wicked man!"

"Do be serious. What of the kiss? That was most improper of him!"

Again Elizabeth bowed her head. "Yes, it was, but I cannot fault him for that." She stopped short of describing the effect it had on her. Elizabeth was still sorting out her feelings about that.

"For your sake, I hope all is forgiven if the gentlemen and Mr Bingley's children are coming here tomorrow, otherwise it will be a very long and uncomfortable visit." Jane silently watched her sister. "I have only one last question," she said, rising from the chair. "Would Papa have approved of Mr Darcy?"

"I believe he would."

Jane bid Elizabeth good night, and the door closed behind her. Elizabeth stood for some time, considering all that had transpired. She knew her change of heart was due to her clearer understanding of and appreciation for Mr Darcy's character. He was kind and generous, but he was also steadfast and honourable, argumentative and stubborn, intelligent and teasing.

"Very teasing," murmured Elizabeth, her fingers lightly touching her lips. With a gentle sigh, she went to her room.

Henry was snuggled up under the coverlet, peacefully sleeping. Elizabeth sat beside him, studying his angelic face to find the resemblance to her late husband.

As the years slipped away, so too had the images in Elizabeth's memory. There were no portraits to remind her of Edward. For all the intimacy that marriage had brought, their two children were all that remained of his likeness. Cassandra, so like her father in temperament, was serious minded and responsible for her age. Henry was more like his mother, adventurous and with a curiosity that could lead him into mischief. Yet, their father's features were etched in their faces—in the line of Henry's nose, the curve of Cassandra's brows.

Tucking the blanket more closely around her son's form,

Elizabeth finished readying for bed. Letting her hair down, she combed it out, then pinned it up under her nightcap. Facing the mirror, she gazed at her reflection for a moment.

Papa, this time I know you would approve.

THE NEXT MORNING AFTER BREAKFAST, once Jane had taken the children outside, Mrs Bennet felt compelled to draw her widowed daughter aside.

"Before our guests arrive, I want you to listen to me. You have never heeded my advice since you were ten years old, but mark my words, if you do not follow it now, Mr Darcy will look elsewhere. Time is of the essence!" She raised her chin, waiting for Elizabeth to voice an objection.

"Very well."

Taken aback by the ease with which this first step was accomplished, her mother was momentarily at a loss for words. That was soon remedied, however.

"First of all, you should change into a less modest gown. You were married. You know what a man likes to see, so use that to your advantage." Mrs Bennet clucked her tongue disapprovingly. "And do try to be more agreeable. Less arguing, my dear. No man finds that attractive."

Hiding a smile, Elizabeth said in an innocent tone, "I did not pack anything other than these mourning clothes. I am afraid this will have to suffice, but Mr Darcy is aware of our circumstances."

Disappointed, Mrs Bennet had no choice but to accept the situation. "Oh, you will drive me to distraction! You will simply have to make a greater effort to be pleasant and keep your impertinent opinions to yourself!" Abruptly, she changed the subject. "I do hope Mr Bingley makes his offer to Jane soon. That affair is progressing very well, if I do say so myself!"

Elizabeth left to go above stairs and check her appearance before the gentlemen arrived. In the privacy of her room, Elizabeth examined her reflection once more.

She was past the fresh-faced look of her youth. Her figure, however, had not suffered unduly by having two children. In some respects, it had been enhanced. She had to admit that the gown she wore did nothing to accentuate those attributes.

Crossing the room, she looked through the few articles of clothing that had travelled with her, drawing forth one of her favourites. It was an older gown, although its age was not readily apparent. Comfortable and cool, the soft fabric easily slipped over her skin.

The mirror presented a much more satisfactory image. Elizabeth tidied her hair, tucking in any loose strands. Finally, confident her mother would not find fault with her appearance, she quickly peered out the window to see if any carriage was approaching down the road and then went downstairs.

"Is that the one?"

Darcy sighed almost imperceptibly as he heard Bingley tell his daughter, yet again, that the house they were approaching was not their destination. Anne was too young to be expected to distinguish between similar looking cottages, but her brother apparently could, judging by the comments he uttered each time she enquired if their journey was at an end.

When the Bennets' home finally did come into view, Darcy felt a ripple of excitement course through his veins. The pleasure of this sensation lent him more patience for the undisciplined exit by young Charles and Anne from the carriage.

Jane and Elizabeth emerged from the house on the heels of Cassandra and Henry. Over the chatter of the little ones, the invitation to come inside was heard. Bingley called his children to him, so they would enter the house together. Darcy, last through the door, was pleased to be met by Elizabeth, who appeared to have been waiting for him.

"Good afternoon," she said, while the maid took his hat and coat. When they were alone, she drew closer. "I promised to let you know about the manservant you offered to send with us tomorrow." He looked at her expectantly, and Elizabeth smiled softly. "I do not think that will be necessary, since you will be accompanying us."

The teasing sparkle in her eyes made him momentarily forget where they were. After bestowing a warm caress upon her cheek, Darcy realised they were in view, should someone enter the hall. He smiled self-consciously, taking Elizabeth's hand in his and whispering, "What time shall I arrive?"

They settled upon the hour, regained their composure, and joined the others.

The afternoon passed too quickly in the estimation of everyone. Jane and Mr Bingley slipped out to the garden, managing to steal a few moments alone. Content simply to be in Elizabeth's company, Darcy was nevertheless pleased when Mrs Bennet found an excuse to remove herself from the room.

Elizabeth poured them each a second cup of tea, observed that the children were happily occupied, and sat next to him. She easily drew him into conversation, but his attention was less on her words than her manner of expressing her thoughts. At last, she placed her teacup on the side table.

Darcy was startled by the sudden silence as she waited for his reply. "I beg your pardon?"

"I fear my company has become too dull to maintain your interest. Perhaps a change of scenery would be beneficial?

The garden may offer more inducement to keep your attention on me."

"I hardly think that likely," murmured Darcy as they rose to leave.

Elizabeth left her daughter with instructions to look after the younger children and informed her that they would be just outside the door, should anything be needed.

The garden had seen some improvement in the short time since Mrs Bennet had taken charge. There were still some wild, overgrown sections, but the roses had been tamed and the weeds noticeably reduced. A wooden bench was situated near the house so that its occupants could gaze out across the narrow lawn to the roses and flowering shrubs.

Elizabeth continued to walk past the bench, sending a quick glance to be sure Darcy was following. Curiosity soon led him to ask where they were going.

"I know precisely where Mr Bingley and my sister are and did not wish to intrude upon them. We shall have a measure of privacy for ourselves in this corner of the garden."

She stopped by a low section of shrubbery that bordered an unruly tangle of branches laden with brightly coloured flowers. "I was hoping your knowledge of superior blooms could identify these, Mr Darcy."

"You are teasing me," he said with an amused expression. "I must caution you to take greater care, for I do not want to repeat my folly of yesterday." With deliberation, Darcy folded his hands together behind his back.

"You have nothing to fear from me, sir. I am under a vow to my mother that I shall not disagree with you today."

His voice betrayed him with its unsteady quality. "Not at all? How is it possible that you would agree to such a thing?"

"Under duress, I assure you. Had I not quickly agreed upon her first asking, I would have been subjected to a longer lecture on the shortcomings in my behaviour and how it would serve me ill. Gentlemen, I am told, would not find it attractive."

"Attraction," countered Darcy, "comes in many forms." He unclasped his hands, stepping closer and reaching around Elizabeth to pluck one of the flowers from the branches behind her. "This wild rose, for instance, retains the essence of the cultivated variety from which it sprung. The colour is vibrant, the scent delicate, but in this form, there is strength to withstand great hardships that would wither the refined plant."

The small pink petals rested in his palm, the bright yellow lashes in the centre of the bloom reaching upward. Darcy transferred the flower into Elizabeth's hand. "Some would seek to reject the wild rose in favour of more easily managed stock. Another would appreciate those special qualities and resiliency."

Elizabeth studied the tiny flower. "Its fragile appearance is deceiving." She raised her eyes to meet his gaze. "How is it that you come to be so knowledgeable in these matters, sir?"

Darcy abandoned all pretence of restraint. "Elizabeth, I know the path I wish to take, where my future should be and with whom, but I will not take advantage of the promise you made to your mother." Her sharp intake of breath must have confused him. "Have I said something wrong? Have I offended you?"

"No, not in the least!" Elizabeth's frustration was evident, and Darcy watched her with anxious curiosity. "Oh, I wish I had not made that promise. It was very selfish of me."

She boldly moved closer until he could feel her heartbeat across the brief distance separating them. "I had hoped for you to repeat your transgression, and my vow would prevent me from reacting as foolishly as I did yesterday."

It took but an instant for Darcy to consider his next

action. He had imagined this moment more times than he could count, but the reality of it sent his heart racing. The warmth of Elizabeth's breath was on his cheek as his lips lowered to taste the sweetness of hers. Her response was as startling as it was pleasurable, encouraging Darcy to draw her closer. To his increasing delight, Elizabeth's arms wrapped about him, further demonstrating a desire matching his own.

Neither Darcy nor Elizabeth was aware of anything else in those moments, least of all the audience they had.

Mr Bingley gently drew Jane from the scene, the shock still evident in her expression. Once she was safely seated on the bench next to the house, he took her hands between his own to warm them.

"Do not be alarmed, my dear. Darcy has nothing but honourable intentions, I assure you." He continued to observe her as his words had their desired effect. "Your sister knows what she is about. I am sorry that you have been upset by witnessing what should have been a private moment for them."

"I am truly not distressed. As you say, Lizzy knows what she is doing, and I have no doubts about Mr Darcy's intentions."

Softly biting her lower lip, Jane paused before whispering, "Would you kiss me like that?"

CHAPTER 21

THE TRUNKS WERE LOADED, AND THE CARRIAGE was on its way. Mrs Bennet bid a tearful farewell to her daughter and grandchildren, conferring upon Mr Darcy the responsibility for their safety. The journey would not be long and the roads were safe, but he nodded agreeably and accepted the charge.

Jane and Elizabeth embraced one another, whispering their goodbyes and a parting word of advice. The prior evening had been spent sharing hopes, secrets, and special memories.

Elizabeth seemed disappointed to see him mount his horse for their departure, but Darcy quietly explained that even the presence of the children in the compartment would not prevent her from tempting him. He insisted it was wiser to avoid any risk of impropriety by riding alongside the carriage. Elizabeth had laughed at him, and the delight he found in it further emphasised the necessity of keeping a proper distance.

It was not long before Darcy noticed Henry watching him through the window of the carriage. He guided his horse closer, so he could ask the boy what he found so interesting. Suddenly shy, Henry ducked out of sight. Darcy looked questioningly at Elizabeth.

"Henry is afraid to ask if he might ride with you for a little while," she said. "Do not agree if you would rather not."

Darcy had no intention of denying the young boy the experience. He called to the coachman to halt the carriage and promptly invited Henry to join him. The footman lifted the boy into the saddle in front of Darcy, who had shifted his position to make room. He nodded to the servant who returned to his seat beside the coachman. They proceeded at a slower pace while Henry grew accustomed to the motion of the horse.

Darcy was perfectly aware of Elizabeth's scrutiny, although he hoped that Henry's excitement, evident from his smiles and laughter, would put her mind at ease. The lad was full of questions, indicating he had not had many occasions to ride. Eventually, the questions ceased, and after an extended period of silence, Darcy realised the boy was falling asleep.

"It is time for you to return to the carriage, Henry," he said. "You are tired."

"Not tired," argued the boy as he yawned.

Once Henry was safely back inside the compartment and they were on their way once more, Darcy resumed his place close beside the vehicle. The window next to Elizabeth was open, allowing them to converse freely. She identified various landmarks as they progressed, describing the history of the area and some of the people who lived nearby. These titbits of information were welcomed by Darcy, as they gave him better insight into Elizabeth's life away from her mother and sister.

Her knowledge of the neighbourhood and her neighbours indicated a woman capable of distinguishing between useful information and idle gossip. It was not that he doubted her discretion, but to have such tangible proof only reinforced his confidence in her future success as mistress of his estate.

The time passed quickly when there was conversation, and soon they reached Elizabeth's home. Darcy dismounted in time to hand the lady down from the carriage while his servants saw to the trunks. Elizabeth's maid appeared at the cottage doorway, mouth hung open in astonishment when she saw her mistress emerge.

"Such a fancy carriage!" she cried before realising that there was a gentleman beside Elizabeth. "Oh, beggin' your pardon, sir!" She dropped a hurried curtsey and lowered her gaze.

"Jenny, please show the footman where to place the trunks," Elizabeth directed, "and then we would like some refreshments as soon as you can prepare them." As the servants disappeared into the house, she reminded Henry and Cassandra to go inside and wash their hands and faces.

Darcy drew Elizabeth a few steps away from the open door. Now that they had reached their destination, he was keenly aware of how little time remained to spend in her company.

"I cannot stay long. It would not be wise to provide fuel for gossip."

The lady's disappointment was visible in her eyes. "I understand, but will you at least stay long enough for a cup of tea? It will be a long ride back to Netherfield. I can have Jenny pack something for you to take along if you prefer."

The offer increased his admiration for her. Smiling in

agreement, Darcy wished for more privacy than he suspected was available where they stood. With the children and the servants in the house, he knew there would be no other opportunity to speak unobserved, and the few moments granted them had to serve his purpose.

"Elizabeth," his voice was low, her name a caress, "I cannot leave you without reaching an understanding between us. If it is too soon for you to answer, please do not hesitate to say so." Darcy paused a moment to inhale deeply. "I love you, dearest Elizabeth, and I would be honoured if you will consent to marry me."

The answer was immediate, the assurance with which she agreed to his offer surprising him. "Yes, I will marry you! I need no time for further consideration. We are neither young nor naïve, sir. We know what we want. At least, that is what you told me the other day, and I am sure of my own feelings! I am delighted at the prospect of becoming your wife."

He brought her hand swiftly to his lips. As he bestowed a tender kiss upon her soft skin, his gaze locked with hers, Darcy allowed his eyes to convey the depth of his emotion, but the husky tone of his voice betrayed how much his control was being tested.

"I shall now be able to endure the coming week without the prospect of seeing you daily. Dearest Elizabeth, you have made me the happiest of men."

Reluctantly, he released her hand but not her gaze. The desire to take her in his arms was almost overpowering, but they were in public view, and Darcy would not risk her reputation.

"Tomorrow morning I shall go to London to begin the necessary preparations. Will you write to me there? I shall require that to sustain me until I return to you."

"Of course I will write to you every day! Oh, and if you will allow me a few minutes, I shall write to Jane and my mother, informing them of the happy news, so they may share in our delight. Will you take my letters with you today?"

"I am powerless to deny you anything," he confessed, voice pitched intimately. "Whatever you may desire, speak and it shall be so. I am yours to command."

He saw Elizabeth's eyes widen with surprise, then soften as her lips curved upward mischievously.

"Follow me," she said and walked towards the side entrance of the house. Continuing around the corner, Elizabeth slipped between the wall and a tall hedge, and led Darcy to a space well sheltered from view.

Elizabeth turned to face him, an eyebrow raised in challenge. "Very well, sir." She stepped closer, raised her chin, and whispered, "I desire a kiss."

He captured her lips, warm and sweet, with the fervour he had been forced to repress mere moments before. His arms enveloped her soft form, drew her closer, and only then did his kisses pause long enough for him to murmur, "I love you so dearly." Darcy's lips followed the curve of her cheek, lingering briefly below her ear, before Elizabeth's head turned and her mouth met his again.

Where her hands rested on his chest, Darcy felt the heat of her touch even through his clothing. With regret, he ended the kiss, loosened his hold on Elizabeth, and leaned against the wall behind him. Her body relaxed into his, her head resting on his shoulder.

"You are not making it easy for me to leave."

She made a sound, suspiciously like a giggle.

Darcy knew they could stay no longer in this private seclusion, however much he wanted to prolong it. He took Elizabeth's hand, pressed his lips to her fingers, and they made their way back to where the carriage waited.

Voices soon announced the return of the servants, and

Elizabeth again issued the invitation to come inside for refreshments before leaving, but Darcy declined. Upon the lady's insistence, he consented to have a basket prepared to supply him and his servants with food for the journey. While Jenny attended to that task, Elizabeth reluctantly left him to quickly pen letters to Jane and Mrs Bennet.

Cassandra and Henry wished to say goodbye to Mr Darcy, and without any prompting from their mother, thanked him warmly for lending his carriage for their trip home. Henry quietly expressed a hope for another opportunity to ride with him soon. A large basket was placed inside the carriage and a smaller one handed up to the coachman.

Elizabeth held out her two letters. "If you would please see that my mother and sister receive these, I would be most grateful." There was little that could be said in the presence of so many people. They had to be content with simple words and innocent looks.

Darcy nodded as he accepted the letters. "I shall be pleased to be of service, Mrs Matthews."

It was not easy to leave her without another affirmation of his constancy. In spite of what had already been said, there was much more Darcy wanted to say. On the ride to Nether-field, he attempted to occupy his mind with the details to be arranged while in London, but his thoughts inevitably returned to the lady he left behind.

BINGLEY WAS ROUSED from his musings by the sound of footsteps approaching the study door. At the knock, he called out to enter and was pleased to see his friend had returned. His first impulse was to ask if the journey passed without mishap, but one look at Darcy forestalled that question.

"She accepted you!" Bingley cried, laughing when the other man's expression changed to shocked surprise.

"How did you know?"

"How could I *not*? Look in a mirror, man! There is no disguising it."

"Well, then I shall admit the truth." Darcy's smile knew no restraints now. "Elizabeth has, indeed, consented to marry me." He pulled the letters from his pocket and handed them to his friend. "These are for Miss Bennet and her mother. As I shall be off for London first thing in the morning, I would be grateful if you would deliver them."

"London? You are wasting no time."

"There is much to arrange." Darcy studied Bingley. "I suspect you will not waste time in my absence, either. I do not expect to return until the end of the week, and then, if convenient, I may take Charles and Anne with me to call on Elizabeth."

"Yes, a week will be perfect." Bingley fingered the letters in his hand. "I am sure Mrs Bennet will be properly distracted for a while by the contents of these."

Darcy agreed completely, then excused himself to go upstairs and change from his travelling clothes.

Bingley called after him. "Darcy, have you eaten? I have already dined but—"

"No, thank you. I am not hungry."

In truth, he had not felt inclined to eat since leaving Elizabeth. The contents of the basket she had sent with him had not been touched. Darcy was too consumed by the business that awaited him and the recollection of their intimate moments before parting to think of anything else. After washing and changing, he sat down at the desk in his bedchamber and drew forth a fresh sheet of paper from the drawer.

At first, the words would not come. There was much that needed to be said, questions he had forgotten to ask, and answers only Elizabeth could provide.

Finally, he took up his pen.

Dearest Elizabeth,
I cannot express in mere words how honoured I am that you
have agreed to be my wife. Apparently, my joy is visible.
Bingley realised our news the instant he saw me.

Sleep shall elude me until I have conveyed the depth of my
regard. My heart is too full to remain silent. Elizabeth, I
would marry you tomorrow if that were possible! Alas, it is
not, for practical matters prevent such an expeditious resolu-
tion. You are, perhaps, laughing at my impatience. How I long
to hear your laughter at this moment!

A soft knock on the dressing room door interrupted him as his valet announced his entrance. The master's night clothes were laid out, the bed turned down, and Wilson stood quietly nearby.

Darcy at last glanced at him. "Thank you, Wilson, that will be all for tonight."

"Begging your pardon, sir," said the servant, waiting for acknowledgement.

"Is there something else?"

A small tray appeared in his man's hand, a folded paper upon it. "This was in the basket that accompanied you in the carriage, sir."

Darcy immediately left his chair and crossed the short distance to take up the paper and examine it. His name was clearly written in a fine hand. He gave Wilson a sharp glance.

"Fitch brought the basket to the kitchen, and I unpacked it, sir. No one else saw this item." He withdrew the tray, placing it behind his back.

Darcy nodded, carefully schooling his features. "Your discretion is always appreciated, Wilson."

"Very good, sir."

When the door closed behind the servant, Darcy eagerly unfolded the paper, his eyes immediately seeking the signature at the end of the missive. The delicate furls in the handwriting belied the haste with which it must have been written. He savoured each word as he read from the beginning.

Dearest,
Please forgive the brevity of this note. We have not the luxury
of speaking openly, and you will be gone in a moment. I so
want to assure you of the great happiness I feel. I may burst
with the effort to maintain proper appearances!

I have so many questions, and I am sure you have an equal
number. Most importantly, how am I to address you now? Mr
Darcy seems too formal. Your Christian name I heard only
once upon our introduction. Is there a name you would prefer
me to use?

My head is too full to think clearly! I shall write to you daily
until your return.

I hear Jenny coming with the baskets now, so I must stop.

With all my love,
Elizabeth

Darcy laughed softly at the supposed importance of her question. Returning to the desk, he sat down to finish his own letter.

In answer to your query, there is no particular name I prefer.
My friends and relations generally call me Darcy. Fitzwilliam

was my mother's family name, and as such, I have several cousins bearing the same. I shall await with pleasure to learn of your choice, be it one or the other or perhaps something completely different.

As for my own questions, I was hardly five minutes from your door when I remembered so many things I should have asked. Out of respect for your circumstances, I am not certain how long an engagement you desire. That decision is yours, for I am not unfeeling with regard to your bereavement. I shall arrange to procure a licence while in town, but do not feel you must hasten the wedding because of that.

I have entrusted Bingley to deliver your letters tomorrow. I wish to be away quite early, far too early to call on your mother and sister. The sooner the business in London is accomplished, the sooner I may return to you. A week will feel an eternity, I am certain.

My main purpose in town is to draw up the marriage settlement. Have you an uncle or other relation to act on your behalf? I assure you, as my wife, you and your children will want for nothing. The provisions will be generous, for you deserve no less.

I would also like to begin preparations to receive you at Pemberley. There will be some refurbishments necessary, and to this end, I want to make sure the changes will appeal to your taste. I will not rush your decisions, Elizabeth, but these are all things that must be considered in the coming weeks.

I have enclosed the direction for my home in London. Foolishly, I neglected to leave that with you today. I fear my mind was distracted by so many things.

I do not feel like a grown man, Elizabeth. It is as though I were twenty years younger. My thoughts are undisciplined, and it is difficult to concentrate. What I have written is probably incoherent.

I shall anticipate your letters with as much patience as I am able to muster, dear Elizabeth, but I must confess that the time will pass interminably slowly until I am with you once more. Until that time, you will be continually in my thoughts and always in my heart.

I am ever yours,
Fitzwilliam Darcy

Once sealed, Darcy called for Wilson and made a request that the letter be sent with the post in the morning. Feeling more relaxed than he had all day, he readied himself for bed, setting Elizabeth's note on the table at his bedside within easy reach. Before settling down to sleep, he read it again at least three times, never failing to laugh at her question, and the adieu bringing him a sense of serenity that had been long absent.

CHAPTER 22

It felt odd to be travelling the road to Mrs Bennet's home alone, but Bingley was grateful for his friend's timely departure. He had been waiting for this opportunity for several days.

Adjusting his waistcoat for the tenth time, pulling his cravat away from his throat for the twentieth, he then drew a handkerchief from his pocket to wipe his brow.

Bingley chuckled. *If Darcy could see me now, he would take back his words. I cannot possibly appear as confident as he proclaimed this morning.*

Mrs Matthews's letters were on the seat beside him. As the carriage came to a halt, he picked them up and took a deep breath to steady himself.

The Bennet ladies received him warmly, although they were surprised by his presentation of letters from Elizabeth when she had only left the previous day. Both put the missives aside, however, and while Bingley knew the importance of the contents, he was in a quandary how to encourage them to read the letters without divulging the secret inside. He decided that removing himself and Miss Bennet from the house would allow her mother the opportunity to discover the happy news while they were gone.

Jane was more than willing to go walking. The town shops were not far, and there were one or two items she needed to buy. They left the house with the expectation of a pleasant hour in each other's company.

Seeing them on their way, Mrs Bennet returned to her cup of tea and glanced at the letters on the table beside her. A feeling of dread overcame her, and in an instant, the paper was in her hand. Heart palpitating rapidly, she unfolded the letter and began to read.

JANE STOLE a glance at Mr Bingley as he walked beside her. His silence was obviously rooted in unease, for this lack of conversation was unusual to say the least.

"Sir," she said finally, startling him. "I am sorry! I did not mean to intrude on your thoughts. They must be serious to occupy you so singularly."

"They are serious." His expression warmed as she shyly lowered her gaze. "Miss Bennet, I—" Instead of continuing, Bingley took her hand and gently turned her towards him. "I love you, Miss Bennet. I love your sweet nature, your beautiful smile, and the kindness and generosity you show to everyone. Miss Bennet...Jane, please marry me."

She had been holding her breath from the moment he began speaking, and able to exhale at last, her answer came out with a rush of air. "Oh yes! Yes, I will marry you!"

They stood giddily unaware of anything else. The sound of a passing wagon, its driver shouting at them to clear the way, brought them to their senses with a start.

Bingley laughed after assuring their safety. "Oh my sweet Jane, how happy you have made me!"

"I thought this day would never come—that I would never fall in love. To find a man who loves me as much as I love him is a dream come true," she whispered, face alight with joy. "Mama will be beside herself! Oh, I must write to Lizzy with our news as soon as we return to the house." A sudden look of insight came over her face. "Lizzy! Is she—do you know? What did she write?"

Smiling smugly, Bingley took Jane's arm and wrapped it about his own. "I would have preferred you to learn this from her letter, but I do not suppose she would mind if I told you what I know. She and Darcy are engaged."

"Oh, I knew it must be so! It is too much! How happy we shall all be!" Jane's eyes suddenly grew wide and her happy expression disappeared. "Oh, we should not leave Mama alone. She will read Lizzy's news and be overcome by nerves and—"

"I am sure there is nothing to worry about. The maid will see to her, my sweet. Perhaps it would be better if we do not share our own news with her just yet. That truly might be too much for her." His sly grin told another reason for remaining silent.

Jane giggled. "Yes, her nerves may settle down in a few days, and then we can tell her."

The errands were forgotten, and they walked on, having much to say to each other. There was little to be decided at this early stage, for Mrs Bennet was sure to insist on certain details, but they could entertain plans for their future felicity.

Bingley's children would certainly be excited to welcome Jane into their family, and she was just as eager to take them under her wing. A trip to London had to be arranged, so Jane could choose the fabrics and wallcoverings to decorate her rooms to her liking. Bingley would accept no demure refusals, for Jane's natural modesty prompted her to deny any need for a change. Her betrothed insisted that her apartments would reflect solely her preferences.

They paid no heed to direction, but from habit, they soon found themselves on a familiar path that led to a favourite spot. There, they finally attained the privacy any newly engaged couple sought.

Bingley spoke in a soft voice. "You asked me something the other day, something that I was not ready to answer in the form you desired."

"I have not changed my mind, if that is what you want to know."

"That is precisely what I wished to hear." Bingley brushed a stray lock of hair from the edge of Jane's brow. "May I kiss you now?"

She nodded slightly, and he could feel her tremble in his arms. Their lips met, she leaned into him, and Bingley pulled her closer. His heart filled with a warmth long absent, and it made him eager to prove the strength of his affection. Yet, he controlled that impulse for this first kiss, allowing his lips to caress hers tenderly before pulling back to observe her reaction.

Jane's eyes fluttered open, eventually focussing on him.

Amused, Bingley grinned. "Jane, my love, you must remember to breathe."

"I shall try to remember. Perhaps with more practice, I shall improve."

"Of that I have no doubt," he assured her, bestowing another kiss upon her waiting lips.

BINGLEY WAS unable to inform his children of their plans, for they would not be capable of keeping a secret. Thus, it was four full days before the news became known to anyone else. The happy couple enjoyed that time, hours spent together while Mrs Bennet fretted over how Elizabeth would manage to plan her nuptials without her mother being present to organise it. Jane learnt much during that time. She knew what to expect when the announcement of her own engagement was made public.

More than one letter had been exchanged between the sisters since the first containing Elizabeth's announcement had arrived with Mr Bingley. Jane had sent her own reply to convey her immense joy at the news and to offer her assurance that their mother was not suffering unduly from the lack of direct involvement.

When Mr Bingley arrived in the morning, he brought with him the news that Darcy would return the next day. He had completed the necessary business in London and was awaiting but one confirmation that, once in his possession, would allow him to leave London immediately.

"At last!" cried Mrs Bennet. "Now we shall have some answers and be able to complete the arrangements."

"I am sure Lizzy and Mr Darcy have already communicated their wishes to one another and preparations have begun." Jane looked to Mr Bingley for confirmation.

"Darcy wrote that he has obtained a licence and that Mrs Matthews has been writing faithfully to him while he was in town. I am certain they have not had much time to write to anyone else, and that is why you have not heard of their plans."

Mrs Bennet's attention seemed to focus on his first few words. "A marriage by licence!" she crowed. "Oh, thank goodness the girl has finally seen sense!" She took Bingley by the arm, speaking to him as she would one of her own children. "Not that there is anything wrong with a traditional engagement period and wedding, of course, but neither of them is getting any younger, and both have been married before. Why wait?"

"Why indeed?"

"This is such happy news! I must write to my sisters at once!" As she hurried away to her rooms, Mrs Bennet happily continued. "A licence! It is perfect, just as it should be."

Jane smiled apologetically. "I can understand why Lizzy would choose to avoid any prolonged period during which our mother would inevitably attempt to have her way."

They looked at each other in silence for a moment. Then Bingley spoke. "Jane, do you think we should–"

"Obtain a licence?"

He took her hands, speaking with sincerity. "Whichever is your preference, my dear, I shall happily comply, but I beg you to consider carefully before you choose. Do not hasten our wedding day merely to avoid the possibility of interference. I am content to have the banns read and to be married in the village church. Your mother's desire is for a perfect wedding for her daughter, is it not? Perhaps your sister and Darcy are not amenable to her efforts, but that does not mean that we should follow their example."

Jane paused to consider the matter. "You are right. Mama may appear overbearing, but my other sisters' weddings were very well planned and executed. I must confess that a few extra weeks will not deter me from marrying you, sir," she said with a teasing smile.

"It is settled, then. We shall take our time and welcome Mrs Bennet's proficiency in these matters."

"Shall we tell her today?"

"No, not today. I think tomorrow or the next day will suit just as well," chuckled Bingley. "Darcy must be granted the privilege of her doting before we draw her attention away!"

· · ·

WHEN BINGLEY RETURNED HOME that evening, Darcy had arrived during his absence. The anticipated document had been delivered earlier than expected, allowing him enough time to make the trip to Netherfield before the hour grew too late. Bingley found his friend comfortably situated in the library, a glass of port in one hand and a book in the other.

"Ah, Bingley, at last!" he said, setting the volume aside. "Have you anything to tell me?"

Laughing, Bingley poured himself a drink, filled Darcy's glass, and sat down. "We shall remain brothers. Jane has accepted me."

"Excellent!" Darcy slapped his hand on the arm of the chair. "How has Mrs Bennet taken the news?"

"Ah well, we have not yet informed her. We thought it inconsiderate to intrude on your moment of triumph," Bingley returned drily.

"Coward," muttered his friend.

"Hah! So says the man who fled to London rather than face his future mother!" They both laughed. "No matter, tomorrow Mrs Bennet will happily make up for the time she has lost in impressing you with the need for her assistance for your nuptials."

Darcy sighed. "I shall make that visit as early as possible and stay as briefly as politely permitted. Elizabeth commands my presence for the rest of the day."

"I cannot blame you for that, and the least I can do is provide a distraction for you, since your engagement provided one for us this week."

They discussed the plans for the following day while enjoying another glass of port. The two gentlemen and Bingley's children would visit the Bennets, after which Darcy would take Charles and Anne when he continued on to Elizabeth's home, thus giving Bingley the opportunity to increase Mrs Bennet's happiness.

The day was destined to be eventful for both of them, and with that in mind, Darcy and Bingley bid each other good-night, their heads full of anticipation for the morrow.

CHAPTER 23

"Come in, come in, Mr Darcy!"

Mrs Bennet practically quivered with excitement when she was at last able to speak to her future son. She reached forward to take his hand and led him into the sitting room, offering him the most comfortable chair before sitting down in the one next to it. Jane and Bingley engaged young Charles and Anne in a game of identifying flowers and birds as they looked out the window into the gardens.

"You can have no idea how amazed I was to read Lizzy's letter last week—that she could write so easily about your engagement when I know she must have been overcome with emotion, especially when you had to leave for London immediately!"

"Yes, she—"

"And she wrote to you there, I understand. How fortunate for you both! Being apart is so difficult when you are newly engaged. I trust everything was accomplished to your satisfaction?"

This time Mr Darcy merely nodded, allowing her to continue uninterrupted.

"Well, I am ready to assist you with anything, anything at all. Lizzy can tell you, I have arranged four of my daughters' weddings, and nothing went amiss. Now, what date have you chosen? How much time do we have to get it all in order?"

"That is what I shall discuss with Elizabeth this afternoon."

"Oh, Lizzy will not allow herself enough time for choosing her gown—the fabrics, the sewing of it! Please remind her that these things do not happen overnight."

"I shall endeavour to keep her mindful that time is limited."

"Then there is the breakfast menu—the cake. Oh, and we must invite guests!"

There was no stopping her now that Mrs Bennet's mission was underway. Mr Darcy did insist that the ceremony was to be small and intimate, as both the bride and groom had previously been married. This engendered some disappointment for her, but she soon recovered her former spirits.

Within an hour, Mr Darcy was prepared to leave. Mrs Bennet found it flattering as well as amusing that he was impatient to see Elizabeth. This sign boded well for her daughter's future happiness and security. The fact that the Bingley children accompanied him also brought her a measure of satisfaction, for it proved he would be considerate of her grandchildren's welfare.

When his carriage was out of sight, Mrs Bennet turned to Mr Bingley and asked, in a manner that required no answer, whether he would stay to dine that evening. That detail being settled, the three of them returned to the sitting room.

With Jane and Mr Bingley established on the settee, the most considerate thing for Mrs Bennet to do was to direct her attention to the letters she had been writing to her younger daughters. Written correspondence had not been a favourite for the youngest, Lydia, and thus there was much to be asked, and the question of her attendance at the impending wedding was of utmost importance.

GRATEFUL THAT ANNE had fallen asleep half an hour into their journey, Darcy was nevertheless plagued with numerous enquiries from his nephew. After initial questions pertaining to the expected duration and distance of their travel, Charles became curious about the places and objects they were passing. There were villages with small shops, grist mills, and smithies, each one holding a mysterious secret for the boy. Darcy knew little about the area, but he was at least able to satisfy Charles with simple facts.

Soon, Elizabeth's house was in sight. As the carriage slowed, Anne awoke, rubbed her eyes, and gave a wide yawn.

The children were suddenly shy in the new, strange place. Darcy was the first to exit the carriage, greeting Elizabeth with surprising composure. Charles held Anne's hand, and they smiled at Henry, until Cassandra, in a perfectly grown-up voice, bid them all come inside out of the afternoon sun.

Refreshments were already laid out on a table, providing some immediate distraction for the children as they busied themselves with the treats. This gave Elizabeth and Darcy the opportunity to speak uninterrupted.

"Have you informed the children of our impending marriage and the changes that will follow?" Darcy asked.

"I have. They were full of questions, of course. They really have no understanding of what it means for them, apart from moving to a new house."

"Perhaps we should both speak to them to explain it more clearly?" Darcy was ready to accede to her greater experience in the matter, but at the same time, he was eager to begin his role as their father.

Elizabeth agreed, and since the children were already settled in chairs enjoying their biscuits, there was no better setting to address them.

Looking at her children, Elizabeth began. "I spoke with you earlier about the changes soon to come."

Cassandra was quick to respond. With a glance at Darcy, she said, "Yes, Mama. You will marry Mr Darcy, and we shall all be moving away from here."

"Correct, but do you understand what else will change?" Elizabeth observed the blank looks on all four children's faces. She smiled to assure them, and she took care to speak in a low, soft voice. "All four of us will live together in Mr Darcy's home."

"Pemmerly!" cried Anne.

"Yes, at Pemberley," confirmed Darcy, rewarding her with a smile.

"And," continued Elizabeth, "Mr Darcy will become your papa."

Cassandra absorbed this information silently, her small brow furrowed in thought.

Henry, however, appeared uncertain. With eyes fixed on Darcy, he whispered to his mother, "I do not understand."

"Our father, silly," his sister loudly whispered back.

Elizabeth gave her daughter a stern glance, then turned her attention to Henry. "Your father died before you were born. Cassie may remember him, but only a little because she was very young. When Mr Darcy and I marry, the four of us will be a family."

"As your father, I shall be responsible for your welfare, your education, and your needs." Darcy paused, his next words bringing the most pleasure for him. "Your mother will be my wife, and you will be my children, too."

Even these simple explanations contained more than young children could be expected to fully comprehend, but the uncertainty had cleared from Henry's expression, and Cassandra left no one in doubt of her excitement at the news.

"That was much easier than I anticipated," a relieved Darcy said once the children had returned to their play. "I do not know exactly what I expected, but their quick acceptance of what is to come is reassuring."

"You have already established yourself as a father in their eyes, especially with Henry. That is an excellent beginning."

"You may be assured I intend to improve upon it." The pleasure he felt at her words reinforced his appreciation of the responsibility he would soon assume. "I am unable to place Henry before Charles as my heir, you understand, but I have some smaller properties, one of which could be settled on him and another on Cassandra as part of her dowry."

Elizabeth's countenance reflected her shock and surprise. "Clearly, you have given more thought to the details than I had imagined. That is most generous of you, sir. There are not many who would consider another man's children so deserving."

"They are your children, Elizabeth. When we marry they will be my children, too." For a moment he merely held her gaze, then gently took her hands in his. "God willing, we may be blessed with more."

The intimate turn their discussion had taken instantly brought colour to her cheeks and tempted his thoughts in a direction too dangerous to entertain. Darcy brought her hands to his lips to place a gentle kiss upon her fingers. "Dearest Elizabeth, how I missed you while I was away."

"Your letters left me in no doubt of your feelings, sir, and on the chance that my own were not clear..." She stopped and glanced towards the children. "I did not realise how strong my feelings were until we were parted. Must you stay at Netherfield until the wedding? It is such a long ride here, and you will spend most of the time travelling to and fro."

"I have no objection to the travel, Elizabeth."

"But I shall worry about your safety, for you will surely be exhausted after several days of that. In the village there is a small inn. It is rather ordinary, but—"

"If it will set your mind at ease, my dear, I shall stay there." The idea was appealing. It would allow more time with his beloved, and Darcy felt it no hardship to suffer a lack of comfort for that pleasure. "Not tonight, of course. I must take the children back to Netherfield. Tomorrow, however, I shall arrange accommodations at the inn and return here as early as possible."

"Thank you." Her eyes said much more than the words could. They were silent for a moment, until Elizabeth asked with some amusement, "Did you enjoy your visit with my mother this morning?"

Darcy smirked in reply. "I have been instructed to advise you to allow enough time before the wedding so that you may be properly attired."

She laughed softly. "Oh, my gown is already chosen and will be completed with time to spare. It is so much easier when there is no need to fuss with extravagance."

"Are you sure that is what you prefer?" he asked, momentarily concerned she was deferring to his wishes.

Elizabeth's laugh put his fears to rest. "I was relieved you wished to forego a lavish affair. Given your place in society, I had expected it to be a necessity, although it would not have changed my resolution to become your wife had you insisted on being married in grand style."

"Every detail will be properly addressed, I assure you.

Our wedding will be on a smaller scale than most would expect, perhaps, but not lacking in style or decorum."

Elizabeth assured him again she was confident that all would be perfect. "We can walk to the church after everyone has eaten. It is not far. Cassandra will see that the little ones do not get into any mischief while we speak to Mr Thompson."

"Is he expecting us?" Darcy thought of the papers in his breast pocket and hoped the meeting with the local clergyman would be completed quickly and satisfactorily.

"He is."

In a few minutes, they were ready to leave. Elizabeth gathered the children together, and they set off. Naturally, there was much to explore on the way, and while the children were tempted to run ahead, a reminder from either Darcy or Elizabeth stayed them from wandering too far.

The church was an ancient stone structure that had seen an addition in the prior twenty years. The grounds were well kept, and its hedges neatly trimmed. Trees towering above the building ensured that the interior would be cooler on a summer day. Mr Thompson met them at the entrance, inviting them to join him inside to discuss their plans.

The entire discussion took longer than Darcy had anticipated, but in the end, all was arranged as he and Elizabeth wished. The walk back to the house was quieter. The children were tired and less active, and the happy couple shared hopes for their future together.

The afternoon waned, and a light meal had been prepared for the guests before they were to depart. As they sat afterwards enjoying their last moments together, young Anne suddenly appeared at Darcy's side with a serious, puzzled expression.

"Uncle Fizzwilly, when will Cassie and Henry come to live with us?"

Darcy drew her closer, taking her hand to say with an equal degree of seriousness, "They will be coming to live at Pemberley after Mrs Matthews and I are married."

The little girl considered that for a moment. "Pemmerly is very big, but Cassie can stay in my room."

"Pemberley is big enough that all of you will have your own rooms," Darcy assured her with a smile.

Thus satisfied, Anne went back to the other children to share her newfound information.

Darcy returned his attention to Elizabeth, only to find her observing him with a mischievous sparkle in her eye.

"Fizzwilly?" she said, one eyebrow arched in amusement.

He started to reply, then reconsidered his words. It would be better to put that particular appellation to rest.

"I know I told you that I have no preference how you address me, Elizabeth, but please do not call me *that*."

MRS BENNET OPENED her eyes to see a worried expression on Jane as she hovered over her. Memory rushed back and Mrs Bennet laughed upon realising she had fainted. She had actually fainted!

"Jane, my dearest child," her mother breathlessly exclaimed, "at last my job is done! All of my girls will be provided for. I need not worry for you any longer."

Jane sighed with relief. "There was no reason for concern, regardless."

Mr Bingley came into view behind Jane's shoulder. "Mrs Bennet, let me assist you to a chair. Perhaps a cup of tea will help to restore you."

Jane got a cup while her mother took Mr Bingley's arm. Comfortably seated, Mrs Bennet accepted the tea and gratefully drank half of it.

"Tell me again, Jane. I think I dreamt it."

"It was not a dream. Mr Bingley and I are engaged." Jane looked at the gentleman adoringly. Mr Bingley returned her gaze in equal measure.

"I do not know where to begin," sighed Mrs Bennet. "We have barely started Lizzy's wedding plans and—"

Jane interrupted her. "We are content to wait until Lizzy and Mr Darcy are married. In that way, you will not feel you are neglecting one or the other of us."

"You are so thoughtful!" She shifted in her seat to be closer to Mr Bingley. "Did I not tell you Jane is the sweetest and most considerate person? After Lizzy is married, we shall plan a spectacular event for you two!"

"That will be perfect." Meeting Jane's gaze over her mother's head, he added, "Everything will be perfect."

A WEEK LATER, Elizabeth looked out her bedroom window at the grey morning. It was not how she had envisioned her wedding day to begin, but it did not dampen her spirits.

I shall soon be married to Fitzwilliam!

How silly it now seemed to believe she needed nothing more than her children and the moderate comfort of their simple lives! It had been enough in the years since Edward died, but Elizabeth's character had not been formed for mere existence.

Her heart swelled as she remembered the past week and the time spent in Darcy's company. There had been a great deal to plan and prepare, but she had learnt so much more about the man she was to marry. They had walked out daily with the children, as much for the exercise as for private conversation. Of course they had spoken of practical matters, but Elizabeth was considerably more affected by the personal revelations and sharing of hopes for the future.

How earnestly—and how often—Darcy spoke of his love for her! The intensity of Elizabeth's own feelings amazed her.

To think I resisted falling in love with the most remarkable man I have ever met. Foolish girl!

She was resolved to show her husband daily that she loved him every bit as much as he loved her.

A light knock on the door interrupted Elizabeth's pleasant musing. Her mother did not wait for an answer before entering.

"Oh Lizzy, my dear, you are not even dressed! You shall be a beautiful sight to behold in your wedding gown. Mr Darcy will not be able to take his eyes off you." Mrs Bennet surveyed the garments laid out for her daughter. "Are you ready for Jenny to assist you in dressing? I shall send for her straight away. Jane is seeing to the children, so you need not worry about them."

Elizabeth was amused at her mother's distracted rambling and cheerfully agreed with everything that was said. Her maid soon joined them, nodding and following Mrs Bennet's directions with the ease of long practice.

THE ACCOMMODATIONS at the modest inn had proved comfortable, if not spacious, but Darcy had been pleased with the convenience of staying near to Elizabeth in the week leading to their nuptials. Despite the expeditious choice of date, the preparations did not feel rushed. As promised, he ensured everything would be as his intended wished.

The previous evening they had said goodnight, stealing a few moments of privacy along with more than a few kisses. Darcy warmed as he remembered Elizabeth's tears at their parting. They were joyful yet bittersweet as he affirmed his love in words meant for her alone. She had responded in kind, sending his heart soaring.

Darcy glanced at his pocket watch and noted he had another ten minutes before he must leave for the church. Wilson had outdone himself preparing his master's wedding clothes. Sitting still and waiting was out of the question, so crossing to the window that overlooked the street, Darcy's eyes quickly focussed on the church a short distance away and his thoughts turned to the solemnity of his wedding vows. This time—this marriage—would be significantly different.

His marriage to Elizabeth would be founded on mutual love and respect. Darcy desired above all else to please her, to protect her, and to love her until the end of his days. This he would avow before God, family, and friends.

The rattle of the door handle announced Wilson's entrance, holding his master's hat and ready to assist with his coat.

"Your work has been exemplary this morning. Thank you, Wilson."

His valet dipped his head in acknowledgement. "Allow me to wish you joy, sir," he said as he slipped the coat over Darcy's shoulders. "I shall await your arrival in London later tonight."

Accepting his hat, Darcy departed the room, his step light and his heart full.

AFTER THE CEREMONY and wedding breakfast, the Darcys' carriage drew away from the town with the newly-wedded couple snuggled together in the compartment.

Mrs Bennet turned to her last unmarried daughter and clasped her hands warmly. "Now we may start the planning for *your* wedding! First, we must speak to the vicar and choose the date. Do you have any preferences?"

Bingley was surprised at the haste she displayed, but he

was just as eager to begin. "Perhaps we might discuss this on the ride to your home," he suggested to a very agreeable Mrs Bennet.

In fact, there was much discussed and decided on the journey. As they had several weeks for preparation, Mrs Bennet stated she was far less concerned with accomplishing everything in that time. She seemed quite confident that all would be ready long before the appointed date.

Bingley saw the ladies to their home and stayed a short time before he had to leave. Letters to his solicitor and his family needed to be written. His sisters required notice before they received their formal invitations. In true Bingley fashion, he had neglected that correspondence in the days leading to Darcy's wedding.

The carriage with the children and their governess had gone ahead, so when Bingley arrived at Netherfield, they had already been given their supper and were ready for bed. Extra rooms had been prepared in advance for Cassandra and Henry, for they would be staying with him until the return of Mr and Mrs Darcy.

Before retreating to his study to take up pen and paper, Bingley went upstairs to bid goodnight to his son and daughter and to check that everything was in order for their guests. All four children were excited to see him.

"Papa!" cried Anne, "Cassie says we are now coozins."

"Cousins, Anne," corrected her father. "Cassie and Henry will live at Pemberley with your uncle and new aunt."

"That makes me happy!" she announced, throwing her arms about Bingley's neck and giving him a hug.

The others were as pleased, if less demonstrative. Henry approached his new uncle. Bingley noted the thoughtful expression on the boy's face and put Anne down.

"Yes, Henry?"

"When Mama comes back, will we have to go home again?"

"No, no," Bingley assured him. "You will be staying here until it is time to go to Pemberley. That is where your new home will be."

Cassandra nodded. "Mama told us that. She said Mr Darcy's home is very far away, but we shall have a carriage to bring us to visit Grandmama often. When she comes back with Mr Darcy, we shall go to live there—with Anne and Charles and you, too."

Bingley chuckled. "I have my own home, as well. It is close enough to allow frequent visits, however," he told them. "The hour is late. We can speak more of this tomorrow. Now, all of you go on to bed."

With some prodding from the governess, the four children said goodnight and disappeared through the doorway to their rooms. Bingley went downstairs to attend to the letters he knew must go out in the morning.

CHAPTER 24

THE HEADY FRAGRANCE IN THE ROOM WAS intoxicating as Elizabeth examined each flower in the arrangement—the blooms full and plentiful and in a variety of colours and sizes. Her husband could not have selected them personally, but there could be no doubt he had a hand in ordering the display.

She gazed about the room, taking in the understated elegance of the furnishings. This was now her bedchamber, at least in their London home. She could only imagine what awaited her at Pemberley.

Elizabeth's cheeks warmed when her eyes settled on the large bed, its linen turned down and readied for the night.

The sound of a door closing startled her, until Elizabeth realised it was her maid leaving the dressing room through the far exit. That brought her gaze to the door that connected the mistress's chamber to the master's and again her cheeks grew hot.

"Take a deep breath," she told herself. "Just relax. There is nothing to be nervous about." In spite of her words, the fluttering of her heart continued. To calm her thoughts, Elizabeth once again approached the flowers, inhaling their aroma.

A colourful tiger moth emerged from one of the blooms and startled her enough to make her cry out. In an instant, Darcy burst through the door in a rush.

"What is wrong?" His eyes searched the room as though he expected an intruder. "Are you well, Elizabeth?" His hands grasped her elbows, drawing her to him protectively.

"Yes, yes," she hurriedly replied. "A moth flew out of the flowers when I bent over the bouquet to smell them. I was merely startled."

Darcy's body relaxed, although his face still showed concern. "I am sorry, Elizabeth. I will speak to the servants to ensure the flowers are more thoroughly examined before being brought upstairs."

"It is not important," she said, a sudden giggle escaping her lips.

"What amuses you so?"

"You must have been terribly alarmed to come in here so quickly." Elizabeth could not resist teasing him further. "What will Wilson think?"

"Wilson?" In another moment he comprehended her meaning. He glanced down to see Elizabeth's palms resting upon his bare skin.

"He may be still standing there with your nightshirt in hand."

The tension broken, Darcy shook his head, wrapping his arms more firmly around his wife's body and drawing her closer. "I am sure Wilson is aware his services will no longer be required this evening."

His whispered reply tickled her ear and was quickly

followed by the brush of his lips. Elizabeth shivered with a delicious sense of anticipation.

"How daring you are to complete your change of clothes without the benefit of your valet."

"'Tis but breeches and stockings, Elizabeth," he mumbled into her neck, "and I have no concern for anyone's opinion but yours."

She felt her feet leave the floor, her weight now resting in her husband's arms as he carried her across the room towards the large four-poster bed. A tiny squeal escaped her lips, causing Darcy to pause momentarily, until reassurance in the form of a kiss urged him on again.

Placing Elizabeth gently upon the sheets, Darcy stood, admiring her as she looked up at him, her smile a mixture of playfulness and desire. Elizabeth raised her hand, extending it in invitation.

Darcy accepted her hand, pressing it to his lips, leaned over to blow out the bedside candle, and slowly lowered himself to lie beside her.

ELIZABETH STRETCHED LANGUIDLY, her senses slowly awakening one by one. The room was dark, except for a bright beam of sunlight that penetrated a small gap where the curtains did not quite meet. The scent of flowers was as fragrant as the night before, bringing recollections just as potent.

The soft sheets were cool against her skin when she moved. Elizabeth snuggled closer into the warmth of her husband's body, tucking her nose under the line of his jaw. He stirred briefly, only long enough to wrap his arms more firmly around her and draw her closer. There was a soft sigh, then his breathing once again settled into a steady rhythm.

She listened to the sound, marvelling at how soothing she

found it. Her hand rested upon his bare chest, feeling the rise and fall with each breath, and she was soon lulled back into sleep.

Waking a few hours later, Elizabeth was pleased to find that Darcy had not left their bed. It may have been the gentle caressing of his fingers on her shoulder that lured her from her dreams. A glance at his face revealed that his eyes remained closed, yet a faint smile played upon his lips as he continued to stroke her soft skin.

"Good morning, Fitzwilliam." Elizabeth barely whispered the words.

Darcy's eyes opened just enough that she could see his gaze focussed on her. His smile, however, was now full, and the hand on her shoulder slipped lower to pull her body tightly against him

"Good morning, Mrs Darcy." His lips rested on her forehead in a soft caress. "Do you like the sound of that as much as I do?"

"Indeed, I would like to hear that every morning when I awaken." Elizabeth lifted her head, inviting a kiss. Darcy did not hesitate, obliging her with more than one.

"Can this be a dream?" she murmured between kisses.

He paused in his attentions but very briefly. "Believe me, my dear, my dreams held no comparison to this."

WITH SIX WEEKS to organise Jane's wedding, her mother dedicated herself to managing every detail. The wishes of the bride and groom were easily satisfied, and when the day arrived, Mrs Bennet was rewarded with the presence of Elizabeth, Mary, Lydia, and their husbands.

Guests filled the church, delighted to witness Miss Bennet and Mr Bingley joined in holy matrimony. At the conclusion of the service, an elegant wedding breakfast was held at Netherfield. Under proficient direction, the servants had meticulously prepared the rooms. The food was plentiful, delicious, and beautifully presented.

Mrs Bennet leaned upon Darcy's arm, her ever-present handkerchief dabbing at her eyes to stem the flow of joyful tears. As Bingley handed his new wife into their carriage, Mrs Bennet broke into a fresh barrage of wailing. Darcy carefully transferred her clutching grasp into his wife's care, an apologetic glance his only defence.

Elizabeth attended her mother, whose happiness knew no bounds. She had seen the last of her daughters properly married, and she congratulated herself on successfully meeting that obligation.

Not one person begrudged the couple the desire to be away as soon as possible, however. Charles and Anne were, of course, a bit distressed when the carriage left, but they were soon distracted by playing with their cousins.

Elizabeth and her mother sought out the company of Lydia and Mary, who had travelled to attend their eldest sister's wedding with their husbands. Kitty had not been able to come, anticipating the birth of her third child. A lengthy and effusive letter had been sent and happily received by Jane.

Recovered sufficiently from her earlier outpouring of emotion, Mrs Bennet vigorously waved a fresh handkerchief to emphasise her accounting of the day. Glancing about the room, Elizabeth discovered that her younger sisters' husbands had rallied around Darcy, who appeared relatively unperturbed by the attention and was politely nodding through their tales.

Lydia asked, "Lizzy, where did you go after your wedding?"

Elizabeth was more than happy to share this news with her sisters. She and Darcy had only just arrived at Netherfield the night before, and had no opportunity to visit with any members of the family.

"First, we travelled directly to London, and stayed at Darcy House for a few days. But then we went on to Derbyshire, to Pemberley."

"Is it as grand as we have heard?" Mary enquired.

"The house is perfectly situated on one side of a valley. I have never seen a place for which nature has done more. There is natural beauty in the landscape, and the park is very large with woods, streams, and hills! I feared we would never reach the house, the ride through the park took so long."

"But the house, Lizzy!" pressed her youngest sister. "Tell us about the house!"

"Pemberley is a handsome stone building. A grand staircase leads to a spacious lobby, a lovely sitting room, and a family portrait gallery. The dining parlour is large and well-proportioned, the other rooms lofty and attractive. The furnishings throughout have true elegance—there is nothing gaudy nor uselessly fine. It is all delightful! From every window there are beauties to be seen!"

"Oh Lizzy!" cried her mother, "that is grand indeed!"

The ladies had many more questions for which Elizabeth happily supplied detailed descriptions of her new home—the number of servants, how many carriages Darcy owned, and most importantly, the respect her husband was accorded amongst his tenants and the local townsfolk.

By the time most of the guests had departed, even Mrs Bennet was too fatigued to speak at any length. Elizabeth wished to retire early, but now that the Bingleys had gone, it fell to her husband and herself to fill the roles of host and hostess to the numerous guests staying the night at Netherfield.

Elizabeth wanted nothing more than to spend some time with her children before the need for sleep overcame her.

Darcy seemed to understand, for he offered a reassurance that he would see to their guests while she visited with the children.

Elizabeth thought it best to check on Charles and Anne first, but upon entering the young girl's room, she found her already asleep. Henry was in Charles's room, the two boys conversing in whispers. She suspected they had begun this ritual the first night Henry had arrived to stay.

Smiling at the thought, Elizabeth walked farther into the room to sit on the edge of the bed. Both boys fell silent, but Henry crawled across the blankets to sit in his mother's lap and wrap his arms about her.

"Did you miss me, Henry?" she quietly asked, holding him close. Feeling his head nod, Elizabeth relaxed her embrace and gently eased him to a position where she could see his face. "I missed you, too." There was clearly something else on his mind, and she smoothed the hair from his brow as she said, "I shall not be leaving you again for a long time."

Surprisingly, this was not what worried Henry. "Must we leave our home and go to Mr Darcy's?"

"Henry, I am now Mr Darcy's wife. His home is mine and, therefore, also yours and Cassie's."

His expression was no less troubled. "Am I to call him Papa now?"

"You may call him Papa or Mr Darcy or perhaps even Father if you like. You need not do so right away, however. Whatever you choose, I assure you he will be pleased."

Henry considered her words, finally nodding as though coming to a decision. With a solemn expression, he looked up at his mother and said, "Thank you for marrying Mr Darcy. Now I shall have a father like all my friends. I shall learn to ride and shoot and be a gentleman!"

"Yes, you will." She was surprised and relieved by his

enthusiasm. "Now, both of you go to sleep. No more talking. You have tomorrow for that." She tucked the blankets around both of them, kissing each lightly on the forehead before leaving the room.

Elizabeth found Cassandra was also still awake and reading a book. Putting the volume aside as soon as she saw her mother, Cassandra demonstrated her delight in much the same way as her brother.

"We were terribly spoiled while you were away. This is such a wonderful house, and Mr Bingley allowed us to eat far too many sweets!"

Stifling a laugh, Elizabeth enlightened her daughter. "You will find a good many things will be different from now on, my dear. We shall be living in a grand house with many servants and wear fine clothes. We shall also have the responsibility to tend to those less fortunate when they are in need. There will be much for all of us to learn."

Cassandra's eyes widened. She found the prospect both frightening and exciting. Her feelings encouraged Elizabeth to remain for some time as they considered the changes soon to come.

EPILOGUE

Twelve years later

ELIZABETH WAS NOT SURPRISED TO SEE HER
husband in a familiar pose at the window in his study. While
she knew the view to be inspiring, it was unlikely to be the
reason for his attention. In a soft voice, she called his name.
Darcy immediately turned, beckoning her to him so that they
stood together, gazing out upon the morning.

"We shall have rain before evening," he said.

Elizabeth studied the sky in the distance, but as usual,
she was unable to understand how her husband could predict
the day's weather.

"They will be gone long before then," she replied, slipping an arm through his. "We are ready to leave."

Darcy drew in a deep breath, held his wife's arm more
tightly to his side, and brought his face down to hers, kissing
her tenderly.

"It would not do for me to cause a delay in the proceedings, then."

They left the study, entering the hall just as Cassandra emerged from the morning room to meet them. Elizabeth released Darcy's arm and watched as he continued forward to take his daughter's hands, smiling proudly.

"You are beautiful, Cassie," he said. "Only one bride has ever been more beautiful—your mother."

Cassandra blushed at the compliment. "Papa, you always know exactly what to say."

They walked out together to the waiting carriage bedecked with flowers and ribbons. Many of Pemberley's servants had come to see the young bride on her way to the church, lining the walkway and the cobbled drive. Darcy proudly handed his daughter into the carriage, then turned to assist Elizabeth. By the time he joined them inside the compartment, the ladies were comfortably settled.

As the carriage drew away from the house, both father and daughter gazed back at the structure, each lost in thought.

Cassandra gave a soft sigh. "The next time I enter Pemberley I will be a married woman."

Darcy was more melancholy. The last time a bride had been conveyed from Pemberley it had been his sister. Georgiana had been a little older than Cassandra but just as eager to begin her new life. Those memories were bittersweet, and Darcy pushed them aside with some effort.

Instead, he drew on more recent memories—the years spent with Elizabeth since their own marriage. She had brought him more happiness than he could have imagined. Her two children were as dear to him as the three she had borne him.

As though reading his thoughts, Elizabeth smiled at him from across the carriage. Had it been possible, Darcy would have moved to sit beside her, take up her hand, and bring it to his lips.

The carriage suddenly slowed and came to a stop as they arrived at the church. Jolted from his thoughts, Darcy shook his head to dispel the lingering effects and was surprised to feel his wife's hand on his knee. His eyes rose to meet her knowing gaze, sharing a moment of deeper understanding.

"Oh, the children are adorable!" whispered Cassandra, seeing her sister and cousins awaiting her in the churchyard.

Darcy stepped down from the compartment first, Elizabeth following, before the footmen moved closer to assist Cassandra. Safely on the ground, Elizabeth and Anne flounced and arranged her skirts, the children assembled to precede the bride's entrance, and Darcy took up his position at her side.

Elizabeth whispered a few words to Cassandra, then paused a moment to observe them all before going inside the church. She greeted Mr and Mrs Lockhart, the groom's parents, and quickly took her seat beside her mother and her sons Henry, Fitzwilliam, and Johnathan.

The young girls scattered their flowers on the church porch in anticipation of the start of the ceremony. Their baskets empty, Jane's girls, Elizabeth and Maria, took three-year-old Georgiana Darcy's hands and led her down the aisle. Following behind, Anne gently encouraged them to take their seats.

Mrs Bennet sighed and brought her handkerchief to her eyes. "Oh Lizzy, how beautiful my granddaughters are!"

Soon, all eyes turned to Cassandra as she appeared on her father's arm and began the slow walk down the aisle to her betrothed. From the moment he stepped inside the church, Darcy was assailed by images from the past—images of his sister with his parents, of his own children being baptised at the font. Sweet but potent, they blurred together until he was suddenly handing his daughter to Jeffrey Lockhart, whom Darcy had witnessed growing from an unruly toddler to a fine young gentleman. Now, nothing more was required of him but to sit beside his wife and watch the remainder of the service.

Elizabeth caught his hand, squeezing his fingers. She was lost in her own whirl of emotions. In spite of herself, she wondered what Edward might have thought if he could have seen his daughter on her wedding day. Cassandra had grown into a beautiful young lady. She vaguely recalled her father in distant memories but had formed a strong bond with Darcy. Elizabeth was often unable to determine if her serious disposition had been entirely inherited or whether she had chosen to emulate the man she called Papa. Darcy had certainly taken earnestly his role in her life. Until the birth of Georgiana, Cassandra had been his one and only daughter to spoil.

In the blink of an eye the service was over. Darcy and Elizabeth stood, their hands joined as their hearts filled with joy at their daughter's happiness. As everyone filed out from the church to make their way to Pemberley for the wedding breakfast, Darcy drew his wife aside to steal a moment of privacy before heading for their own carriage.

"Dearest Elizabeth, thank you for coming into my life and consenting to share it."

She smiled, somewhat amused at his sentimental words. "I believe we have settled this before, Fitzwilliam. I am the thankful one."

He smiled in return, acknowledging the old argument. Softly brushing his lips against her cheek, Darcy wrapped her arm around his and led his wife into the morning sunshine and to the carriage where their sons and daughter awaited.

ACKNOWLEDGMENTS

I want to send a huge thank you to Amy D'Orazio and Jan Ashton, whose unexpected email early in 2021 lit a spark which ignited my dormant muse. My editor Debbie Styne also has my thanks and appreciation for her excellent guidance and corrections. I continue to learn and improve as a writer with their feedback, input, and support.

ABOUT THE AUTHOR

Linda Gonschior has entertained the art of writing since elementary school but never allowed it to come to fruition until *Pride & Prejudice* lured her into deeper exploration of characters, relationships and 'what ifs'. Writing is not the breadwinner, however, as she has a day job and many other interests that compete for attention and time. Still, she has managed to squeeze in several dozen stories–long and short– and there are many more in the 'incomplete' folder on the computer. As retirement looms on the horizon, some may be dusted off to evaluate their potential to entertain those who share a fondness for Jane Austen's characters and don't mind straying a little off the beaten path.

Amongst her accomplishments Linda counts raising a son, stage managing live theatre productions, flower gardening, and website administration, but not netting purses or painting screens.

ALSO BY LINDA GONSCHIOR

Reflections

When Will Darcy finally succumbed to his feelings and proposed to Elizabeth Bennet, he had no idea what he'd started.

Scorning his feelings and refusing to believe any good of the man, she summarily dismissed him as deluded, and that in no time at all his love would be forgotten.

Stung, Will began a path of self improvement that would eventually prove to Elizabeth that he was worthy of her love. A perfect ending was within reach when a family crisis and misunderstandings interfered, separating the couple and leaving one with a secret that will change both of their lives.

Inspired by Jane Austen's most beloved couple, *Reflections* takes a modern journey through mistaken opinions, wounded pride and discarded prejudice.

A Tarnished Image (Reflections Book 2)

Is there anything more perfect than a romantic wedding and a honeymoon in paradise? The happy ending that began in *Reflections* continues as Elizabeth and Will Darcy settle into married life. Their rambunctious two-year-old son, Elizabeth's new job, a meddling mother-in-law, and Will's daily lessons about fatherhood are among the inescapable challenges that are simultaneously frustrating and amusing. The newly married couple discovers the complexity of family life and their need for one another when past ghosts unexpectedly return, casting a shadow on the happy life they are building.

Parallels (Reflections Book 3)

Love, heartbreak, and self-discovery are life's greatest challenges, no matter who your parents may be.

Will and Elizabeth Darcy faced those challenges twenty years earlier, yet marriage taught them patience, understanding, and most importantly, the irreplaceable value of one another. Now their children are about to embark upon that path, hopefully to learn those lessons more gently and avoid the mistakes of their parents.

This third book in the *Reflections* series brings to a conclusion the story of a couple whose love drew them together in spite of themselves and continues to test them when least expected.

Made in the USA
Columbia, SC
02 May 2022